FROM **TECHNICIAN** *to* **CEO**:

The Evolution of a High-Growth Pest Control and Lawn Care Company

DANIEL S. GORDON, CPA

25% of the net proceeds from the sale of this book will be donated to: The Valerie Fund, Supporting Comprehensive Health Care Services for children with cancer and blood disorders (www.thevaleriefund.org).

TABLE OF CONTENTS

PROLOGUE

My journey through the service industry started more than 20 years ago. Depending on how you define success, I've found it spiritually and financially. I've worked hard sometimes, tilting the scales the wrong way in terms of balancing my life, but I've always moved back to the center of that scale. I'm thankful to have a family that understands me and allows me to pursue my professional goals without hassle or guilt.

I have a successful business, wonderful family and financial independence. What's next? How about writing a book about what I've learned to share with others. When I spoke to Marty Whitford, editorial director of North Coast Media, about my idea in November of 2012, we agreed it could be fun and we could make a few bucks in the process. I began working on this project soon after, progressing nicely, knowing I'd need to slow the project down during March and early April for tax season when our firm, PCO Bookkeepers, and TurfBooks prepares more than 1,000 tax returns. The slowdown was part of my work plan to help with the tax work. Never did I think I'd slow down for what followed.

On March 7, 2013, my life and the life of my family changed forever. My son Matthew, a freshman at James Madison University who has aspirations of following in his dad's footsteps to become an accountant, asked my wife to make a doctor's appointment because he felt a lump in his neck. Within a few days, the news worsened. The X-ray showed a mass. The next day Matthew was scheduled for a biopsy that showed Hodgkin's Lymphoma. A few days later, several scans showed it spread to several areas of his body. The doctors labeled it stage four.

The news incapacitated my wife, Carol, and me for several days. This is a parent's worst nightmare – anger and helplessness filled our every waking moment. For readers who have kids (and those who don't), this was the unimaginable. Your son-who was an honors student, a three-year varsity letterman in high school lacrosse, a kid who ate properly-was always in the gym and just beginning to live life as a young adult-was hit with this horrible disease.

When something like this happens, there's no shortage of information, misinformation, opinions and decisions that need to be made quickly. Carol, one of the most organized people I know, was able to put together the plan of attack. For anyone who hasn't been through it, cancer is a full-time job – the coordination with doctors, insurance claims, 17 medications that need to be administered to counteract the chemo cocktail, and the severe flulike symptoms after each round.

As a parent, you try to teach your kids to do the right thing, solve problems and succeed in life. For Matt, the student became the teacher. The way he handled the entire nightmare has been nothing short of inspirational. His attitude, sense of humor and strong acumen for moving forward has taught me so much about how it's not what happens in life, but how you handle it.

When the doctors told him to withdraw from school because of his illness, he said he wasn't going to do that because he worked too hard. He would do what he could from home and travel from our home in New Jersey to Virginia for as many classes as he could in between rounds of chemo. Carol and I didn't like it, but as a young adult, Matt had to make his own decisions. Matt not only went back to school, but he earned terrific grades. I'm so proud of him!

The outpouring of help and support from our friends and neighbors was amazing, and I thank everyone wholeheartedly. The varsity lacrosse team at Matthew's high school alma mater wore his number on their helmets and dedicated the 2013 season to him. The team advanced to the state championship tournament that season. You guys are terrific!

Now for the good news. After completing his chemo regiment, his tests read negative, meaning he's officially in remission. And while he'll never be completely out of the woods and need to return for checkups, this is the best possible news.

I started this prologue by saying we did this project for profit. While I've been fortunate enough to succeed in business and be financially secure, this experience has taught me a great deal about myself, my family and those around me. It has taught me to realize that if you think you have a problem and it can be solved with money, it's not a real problem at all. It's just a challenge that can be solved. A real problem is what Matthew went through. So far, he has been lucky. However, during his treatments at Morristown Medical Center, we met so many kids who aren't as lucky as Matthew – kids who have rare forms of cancer that, while being treated for a disease, might not recover. This is more prevalent than most people know.

We go through life viewing it from the paths we walk and the experiences we encounter. Until our paths cross a situation like this, we never really think about issues such as kids with cancer. If we do, it's not something that consumes our thoughts every moment of every day.

While I want so much for our family to move past this experience, I can't help but think about the kids who are going through worse ordeals – cancer that can't be cured, parents who can't afford health insurance, or health insurance policies that don't cover certain tests and treatments.

To do my small part, this project has been converted from a for-profit endeavor to one of hope – hope for the many kids that aren't as lucky as Matthew. Therefore, all profits from this project will be donated to the *The Valerie Fund*. If you'd like more information, please contact them or mail your gift to:

The Valerie Fund
2101 Millburn Avenue
Maplewood, NJ 07040
www.thevaleriefund.org
Phone: (973) 761-0422

PREFACE

This book is about the journey of Peter Hall, a second-generation pest control operator (PCO) and lawn care professional (LCP) who grew up amid his family business, went off to college to earn a business degree and returned home to work in, and eventually take over, the family business. While growing up, he watched his father work diligently to make a modest living for his family. While attending business school, Peter studied several facets of business, including management, accounting, finance, marketing and operations. His professors used the case method to teach, using successful high-growth, highly profitable companies as subjects. After learning about the strategies employed to expand these model companies, Peter believed he was in a position to move his family's pest and lawn business on a high-growth trajectory. But what tools would he need to make this happen? Do the lessons he learned in the classroom translate to a realistic strategy that can be used to grow a company that will dominate the market, creating above-average income and providing long-term wealth for his family?

For more than 20 years, I've been involved with the pest management and lawn care industries as an owner, manager, CFO, consultant and, most recently, the managing member of an accounting firm that caters to pest control operators and lawn care professionals nationwide. Throughout the years and through my association with fellow PCOs and LCPs – who are members of NPMA (National Pest Management Association), PLANET (Professional Land Care Network) and various state associations – I've met many wonderful owners. Many have developed large and successful companies. Many own companies that are smaller but have created a comfortable lifestyle by providing the time and money needed to pursue hobbies, charitable endeavors and quality family time. Many have been in business for several years and still struggle to elevate to the next level.

So what defines success, and how does one achieve it as an owner or manager of a pest or lawn management company? How are so many PCOs and LCPs expanding their companies and keeping themselves challenged as their sons and daughters use modern business tools to build these businesses.

With the information age well under way, business is more sophisticated and competitive than ever. The next generation of PCOs and LCPs, who are different from their parents, are engaged in creating and implementing strategies conceived to move quickly into larger, more profitable enterprises using technology as their beacon.

This book was written to share the thought processes and business tools turning the industry into a well-respected market segment of the economy by those inside and outside the industry who ask the question: "Is there money in bugs and lawn care?" Well, Wall Street has recognized the power of our recurring revenue model and has pooled money to create portfolios of high-growth pest and lawn companies during the past several years. So clearly much of the smart money that used to look past our industry is flowing in.

In the following pages, you'll join Peter during his journey from a young man working in his dad's business to gaining the book smarts by studying a university business curriculum to experiencing the trials and tribulations of growing a successful business to becoming one of the new breed of pest and lawn industry leaders. If you own or manage a pest or lawn care business, you'll learn many of the strategies employed, key performance indicators used and the mindset needed to create a market-leading company.

While there are many informative books about building businesses – each focusing on a specific discipline such as management philosophies or marketing strategies – I'm unaware of a comprehensive book that illustrates what's needed to leverage business tools to build a successful pest or lawn company. This book can serve as a reference for those who are embarking on a journey similar to Peter Hall's.

While Peter's journey is fictional, the examples and illustrations used in his story come from my experience working with hundreds of companies throughout the U.S. during the past 20 years. Some are successful strategies; some are horrible. But all were conceived by entrepreneurs who were building their businesses. My motivation for writing this book is mostly borne by the satisfaction I derive as an accountant and consultant in the industry I love, providing clients and friends with progressive business-building tools and seeing how they employ them to become successful industry leaders.

I'd like to thank my wife, Carol, for choosing to travel life's journey with me. We've had an adventurous ride, and I wouldn't have done it any other way. I love you, honey! I'd also like to thank my kids – Matthew, Melissa and Michael – for being terrific. They're the best children any dad could ask for. I'd also like to thank my business partner and dear friend, Rob Gatti, for his guidance and friendship throughout the years. It's been so much fun. And last but not least, the guy I couldn't have built our business without, the hardest working, most focused individual I know, Anthony Pepe. Ant, you're only getting started in a lifetime full of greatness. Thanks so much.

INTRODUCTION

Why do most entrepreneurs start a business? Perhaps it's ambition, which is the desire for personal or professional achievement. Being an entrepreneur is much more than trying to make a lot of money. It's becoming a leader of people, an innovator who finds better ways of accomplishing things with respect to product or service improvement, or the efficiency with which products are built or services are performed.

But why do some small business owners create businesses comprising of just themselves or perhaps with a few others, while others create businesses with tens of thousands of customers and hundreds of employees with multiple departments representing various service lines and business functions. The answer lies in the owner's strategic thinking or lack of it.

While the story you're about to read might be entertaining, it's value is the way you look at your business. While it takes a roadmap to reach the desired destination, the strategy of reaching that destination must be laid out via a roadmap. Clearly, the desired result of building a successful pest control or lawn care business is the destination, but to do so, you'll need to devise and implement a strategy that you'll need to update constantly to stay on course.

Now for the most important statement in this entire book: *Hope isn't a strategy*. The difference between the thinking of the owners of small and large businesses has to do with what they believe their role in their organization should be. The owner of the large business sees himself as the conductor of the orchestra, with multiple instruments that need to be played in a certain manner for the music to sound right. His role is to look for and train those musicians constantly to improve the music he produces. The owner of the small business sees himself as a musician, perhaps a great one who can play several instruments, but can't transition to conductor.

The small-business owner thinks of himself as the technician, salesman, office worker and go-to guy for every decision or problem that arises in the course of business. The big-business owner forms a staff to handle all these functions. To develop a large organization, you must be able to look beyond the daily battlefield and plan the war so to speak.

That said, I challenge you to read this book and consider it as a building block in your journey that helps you grow your pest or lawn business. Furthermore, I challenge you to be in the mindset of growing your business entity rather than personally performing services. In my experience working with hundreds of clients of all sizes nationwide, this is what separates the small-business owners from the ones who build large businesses. People management, workflow, marketing and money allows a business to grow; and carefully planning and executing this strategy allows an owner to plan for family and leisure time critical to avoiding burnout before the job is done.

"A man should never neglect his family for business."
—*Walt Disney*

MEET THE HALLS:
Are they really running a
pest control and lawn care company?

"OK, it's a deal," said Michael Hall, as he wrote a check to his local Valpak representative. Because of the yellow pages and the cooperative mail packs during the past several years, Green Pest and Lawn Solutions was able to generate enough phone calls in mid-April to backlog enough termite work to last through most of the summer for Michael and Chaz, the company's lead termite technician. Additionally, the lawn care route was full, and Carl, the company's lawn care technician, was finishing the first round of fertilizer applications and trying to set up the second round, as well as dealing with the annual crabgrass explosion. Michael's son, Peter, was in his last year of high school and would often ride with his dad and Chaz to help after school and during the summer.

Years ago during the spring, there was a time in the pest and lawn businesses when advertising in the Yellow Pages would bring 10-to-1 returns and a ton of lawn and pest leads. A carefully timed Valpak coupon that would arrive in people's home in early April was like printing money for the pest and lawn business because that was when termites started their annual reproductive swarms. Customers usually opened the coupon exactly when the termites were swarming. Additionally, it seemed like there was an endless need for lawn care for those who received the mailers.

It was a time when each truck would generate $1,500 to $2,000 a day. Money was flowing for Michael to pay all his bills and have enough left over to provide a decent living for his family. Michael's wife, Linda, would answer the phone, handle the paperwork and do the bookkeeping.

Michael seemed to be making money with just himself, Chaz, Carl, Peter, Linda and a couple helpers. Operating the business seemed easy, so Michael decided it was time to expand it because the phones seemed to get busier each year and the company was turning away work during the season because it couldn't handle the number of phone calls.

During the next year, Peter went off to college to study business because he loved the challenges he saw his dad deal with and was enamored with the idea of growing Green Pest and Lawn into a large company with a significant presence in the market. Michael hired more technicians and purchased a truck to handle the growth. Revenue was increasing briskly. The company grew from $200,000 in gross revenue to more than $750,000 in revenue in a few years. The termite and lawn business kept everyone busy each year from early spring to fall, and calls to manage bees, fleas, mice and other general pests filled in the gaps in the technicians' schedules. The lawn care business provided revenue, too, but many customers skipped service, and scheduling became a difficult puzzle for Carl and Linda because customers were added from all throughout the territory who were sold customized plans that differed from client to client.

On the surface, everything appeared to be great: The business was growing, there were additional trucks on the road, and the phone was ringing off the hook with new business. Green Pest and Lawn was offering 30-day terms to customers who couldn't afford to pay for their service on the spot. Linda was driven crazy trying to schedule work and retreats and complete paperwork, but the company kept generating more work.

At first, this growth seemed exciting. The termites swarmed, the lawn service was sold, the phone rang, the jobs were booked, and the money rolled in. It was almost euphoric. After all, you go into business to increase revenue, profit and the number of employees. That's what business is all about, isn't it?

But what happens when you expand past the point of performing all the work yourself and you aren't set up in terms of know-how and infrastructure to handle all the business? Green Pest and Lawn's problem was that the Hall's were losing their sanity. In the spring and summer, there was too much work and not enough time in a day to accomplish everything. In the fall and winter, there wasn't enough work to keep all the technicians busy, and there wasn't enough money to make payroll. But as Michael explained to Linda, it was the price of success. "The harder you work, the more successful you become," Michael told her.

Green Pest and Lawn Solutions was growing, but was it

growing successfully? Well, during this growth period, an outsider might see it differently. Revenue increased every year, and headcount increased each season, but with different employees, there was never enough cash to pay the bills, make payroll or pay taxes.

Once the company needed more than a few trucks, things changed. To purchase additional trucks, Michael worked with a local bank and became friendly with the banker from the local Rotary Club, who told him what the company's finances needed to be to secure financing in the future. While the company was small and only needed two trucks, the bank basically financed them based on Michael's signature and the fact he was an active member of the local Rotary Club.

However, with growth and the need for more trucks, the bank asked for financial statements prepared by a certified public accountant. Michael took this information to the local bookkeeping service he hired to do his accounting. Not understanding the local bookkeeper wasn't a CPA, the statements she prepared weren't adequate. It was clear Sarah, the bookkeeper who reconciled bank statements and paid bills for a few small businesses, didn't have the accounting expertise to produce financial statements in accordance with generally accepted accounting principles.

While the amount of pest and lawn work was increasing significantly, cash was tight, and it seemed there was always a fire to put out in the office, leaving no time for collection calls to those customers who had outstanding balances. This was extremely upsetting to Linda because she believed customers had a moral obligation to pay their bills within terms and without reminders.

So why don't Michael and Linda have time to plan, collect money and make it home for dinner at a reasonable hour? They're busy growing a business. Busy taking calls, scheduling appointments, doing termite work, running to screaming customers, pulling technicians off one job and putting them on another because of an emergency, running back and forth to Home Depot to buy supplies, repairing equipment, running to the post office, running to the bank, running to a job to unlock the truck of a technician who locked his keys in the truck, attending chamber of commerce meetings. You get the picture. Sound familiar?

Are the Hall's really growing their business? Where do we start when we want to grow a business?

Dan's observations and recommendations

We know the situation: The phone is ringing off the hook, and sales are rolling in. Sure, there are problems, so we bark out orders to let others know how to deal with them. At first, it's within control. Some get lucky and work with a partner or key person that can share the insanity, but we strive to provide what our customers want – quality service at a reasonable price. Once word gets out that's what we provide, we start to grow, and the growth creates problems because we can't be all things to all people. We can't be in multiple places at once. And so it goes.

This is the story I see all too often in my position as an industry consultant. Some owners figure it out and develop their management skills, and some stay on the wheel – like the hamster you had as a kid who'd run and run and run only to tire himself out, take a rest and get ready to run on the wheel again.

It's the ability or inability to create a compelling picture of what the business can become – to find the inner motivation, to craft the plan and devise systems, to delegate and verify tasks needed to grow a business that will determine if a PCO or lawn care professional will expand his business past the stage of the few-person company acting dysfunctionally.

It's all about a plan. The first step is to create a vision for yourself and your business. What will the business look like next year, in five years, 10 years, etc.? The first step is garner the motivation to devise and execute this plan. In the chapters ahead, I'll help develop the plan. But before I write about becoming involved with such a massive undertaking, let me write about the motivation it will take.

We all need motivation

Reaching the next level requires self-reflection and soul searching. Think of the big picture. Your business isn't your life, but it's a large part of it. Think of what you want people to think about when your name comes up. What do you value in life? Who do you want to be? Live your life as if it were important and build your business in a way that helps you achieve your goals in life.

One of the most difficult things to do is step back and remove yourself from the business. Many times we feel we're one with the business. It takes time to mature and learn the business is a mechanism for you to achieve what you want out of life. The bottom line is you want a successful business you're proud of that provide the means by which you can take care of your family. You want to create a lasting legacy to sell some day or pass on to your children.

If you spend 24 hours a day working on your business, you won't have time to reflect on it, which is important because this reflection provides sound ideas for the next phase. Remember, business is a game. It continues, and you have to keep devising a game plan. You have to think about the big picture and how you want to set up your business. You need to focus on what you want to do and how you want to do it.

Balance is the key. Determining the right balance between work and leisure, how you want to structure your daily schedule, and how you want to live your life are important considerations.

Again, your business isn't your life, but it's such a critical part of it, which determines how you can afford to live it? When setting up and operating your business, you constantly have to stay in tune with your core values, who you want to be, and what you want to achieve. Build your business with purpose and energy while keeping your overall goals or the big picture in mind.

How do you see yourself? How do you see your organization? Self-image can affect everything from your goals to how you grow your service business. If you have in mind that you're a certain type of business owner who doesn't want to change, or you're a 200- or 300-customer operation and that's all the customers you feel you can handle, then you're absolutely right. Until you change your thinking and your self-image, you'll have a difficult time expanding your business past its current level.

Let's look at the following specific areas:

1. **Be ambitious, be aggressive, and most of all, be proud!** You must have a high level of confidence and develop aggressive goals. Think about what you want your image to be, and achieve that. Build your business the way you want it to look.

2. **Think about your business and how it looks.** What does your work place look like? Is it a corporate-looking environment, or is it a small shack on the side of the road? Remember, if you want to work somewhere for a long time, you want it to be nice. Do your employees dress professionally, or are they wearing ripped jeans and old T-shirts? How do you dress when you go to the office? Are you setting a good example? These small aspects of a business matter to your clients and your company, but most of all, you'll find these things matter to you and your self-image.

3. **Get over the idea you're the service guy.** When you first entered the industry, people you knew might have

questioned your decision and asked, "You're going into the pest control or lawn care business?" Overcoming the critics around you can be a huge stumbling block.

A word about self-image

It might take time to come to terms with your self-image. You might think of yourself as the service man and ask yourself, "Why am I doing this?" As you meet more business owners in the service business, you'll see there's a lot of money to be made in this business. Perhaps you've already discovered this. Just ask any of the guys who grew up in a family-service business.

A while back, I saw a CNBC news story about closet millionaires in America. The central idea was these millionaires came from unglamorous businesses, such as sheet-metal fabrication and manufacturing. Pest control and lawn care were also among the most profitable businesses that created a number of millionaires. So don't think of yourself as the guy in the truck. You're a business owner, and you happen to be in the pest control, lawn care or other service industry. It's more accurate to think of yourself as the money guy.

Believe you're invincible, and be bold with your business decisions, knowing you're in a profitable business and you're your own boss. If you want to turn your business into a well-respected corporate entity, go about it in an effective, ethical and profitable manner. You've heard the phrase, "Make your mother proud." Well, this time around, do it for yourself. Make yourself proud.

Don't let fear paralyze you from action. Learn to overcome fear. Fear of the unknown will also stunt your business' growth. In some cases, fear can be healthy and isn't always bad, but fear can be a huge problem if it you let it paralyze you from taking action.

When growing your business, it's important you maintain

a positive attitude. Many times, when it's your money on the line and you're taking all the risk, it's difficult. But remember, all outcomes are just results. Don't look at everything as a success or failure. For example, when a successful person tries something and it doesn't work, that's fine. It's called a result. You have good and bad results. Successful people don't see a bad result as negative. It's just new information that can be used to achieve better results in the future. I'm not advocating taking undo risk without regard for the consequences. It's necessary to step out of your comfort zone every once in a while.

Sometimes fear will settle in and make you gun-shy when you learn about the ramifications of a poor decision. As you grow your business, errors can be more costly. An error that might have cost $1,000 in the past might cost you tens of thousands as time goes by and your business expands. It makes sense to surround yourself with intelligent and experienced advisors who can help guide you through difficult decisions, make you feel more comfortable with your business decisions, and keep your fear from paralyzing you and your organization.

Learn to flex those risk-tolerance muscles because fear is a powerful feeling, but don't be afraid to pull the trigger and execute. Every time you have a bad result, think of it more as an opportunity. You don't necessarily have to take huge risks, but you should take healthy, calculated ones. If you don't exercise your muscles, they'll become weak because they're not being used. Taking calculated risks is similar. If you don't take calculated risks, you don't give the muscles an opportunity to work for you. Be a calculated risk taker not a cowboy.

Fear varies for different people in different stages. Early in the game, depending on your personality type, money is likely the focus of your fear. I don't have enough money for this or that. Well, looking back, many entrepreneurs say that if they knew then what they know now, they probably wouldn't have done many of the things they did to succeed. They admit their fears might have held them back had they known they should've been afraid in the first place.

Good entrepreneurs don't always seem to make rational or logical decisions, but they make them anyway no matter what other people say. And this is partly dependent on your personality type and what your fear is. For example, some might ask, "Am I going to get a good return on this investment?" Others in the same situation will say, "Will this bankrupt me?" And some others will say, "What will people think of me?" Take the chance and remember fear varies for different people in different stages. Sometimes your decisions will work out well, and sometimes they won't. The motivation and energy entrepreneurs have can help make ideas and visions come to fruition.

So you might ask yourself, "What if nothing happens?" or "What if it fails?" You might continue to ask questions such as, "Will fear always be a part of the equation." But remember fear can be a stimulant as well. It will drive you to beat your competitors. Fear can provide you with the motivation you need to grow your business aggressively.

You're going to have days when you lose a lot of money because of a decision that didn't work. Consider it initiation or tuition, and make sure you learn from the experience. The key is not to let fear paralyze you. You have to learn to do it. Sometimes you merely need to run your business by your instincts and a carefully crafted plan.

"High expectations are the key to everything."
—*Sam Walton*

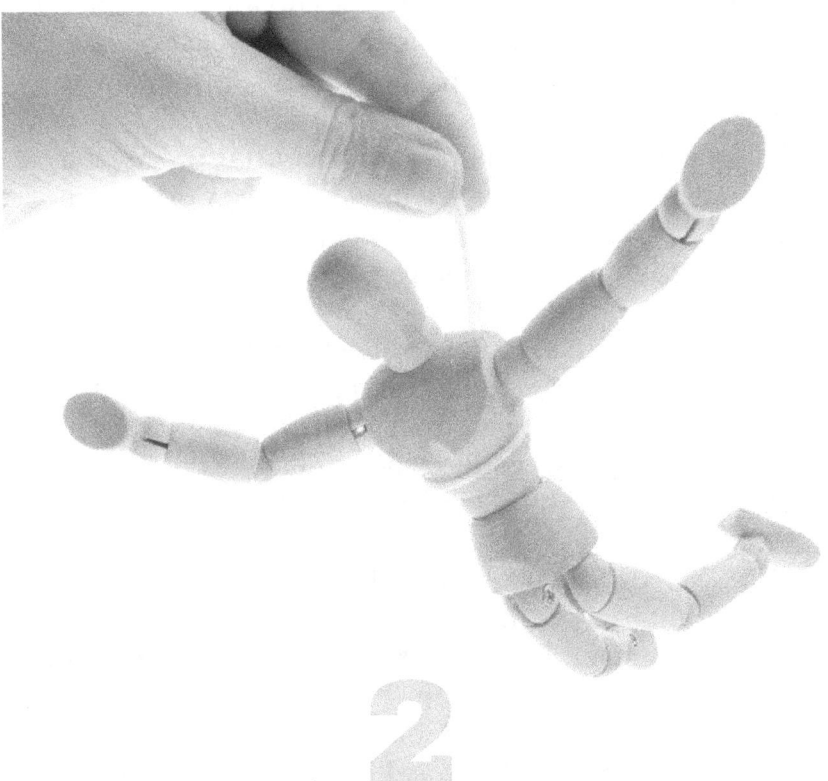

DO YOU RUN YOUR BUSINESS, OR DOES YOUR BUSINESS RUN YOU?

"Mr. Morris, I agree your lawn has weeds throughout and, as you said, there appears to be a bee problem on your deck. Can you excuse me for one second?" "Hello, this is Michael. I know our man was supposed to be there by 1:00 today, Mr. Nugent. Let me see where he is, and I'll call you right back." Michael's phone was on vibrate…and vibrate it did, all day long.

"OK, Mr. Morris here's what I can do for you: I can offer you our multistep lawn care program that feeds your lawn, controls the weeds and keeps the nutrients in your lawn balanced. The cost for this program is $299.00 for the year. Additionally, I'll take care of your bees using an insecticidal dust and give you a 30-day guarantee on the work for an additional $110."

"It's a deal, but I need you to take care of the bees now," said Mr. Morris.

Michael went to his truck for the bulb duster and ladder. As Michael took care of the bees, he couldn't help but think about all the things he had to take care of, from calling customers back to scheduling the new sales he made to ordering material. But, as he reasoned, this is the life of an entrepreneur.

"Mr. Morris, I've taken care of the bees," Michael said. "If you want to write me a check for that and half of the lawn care program, I'll have the office set that up. Thanks so much. I'll be in touch."

Michael felt the familiar vibration from his phone. "Hello, this is Michael." It was Linda. "Can you stop by the distributer? Chaz's pump is leaking, and he needs a new gasket." "Aren't there any in the shop? Why doesn't Chaz have an extra on his truck?" "Well, he said he's been asking you to service his pump for weeks," Linda said. "I know, I know, Linda. I've been busy servicing, selling and trying to keep customers happy. Oh shoot. Linda, can you get Chaz over to Mr. Nugent's place? He called me and said we were supposed to be there by 1:00." "Michael, Mr. Nugent isn't on the schedule until next Tuesday," Linda said. "No, no Linda," Michael said. "I put him in the computer myself. "Hmmm …" Linda said. "The problem is you put him in for next Tuesday, not this Tuesday." Oh, boy!

"Hello, Mr. Nugent." "This is Michael from Green Pest and Lawn Solutions. I have a problem. Our office scheduled your pest control next Tuesday instead of today. A screaming Mr. Nugent replied, "I took the day off from work to be here so I could show you exactly where the problem is, and if you guys aren't here in the next 15 minutes, don't bother coming." Click. Mr. Nugent hung up.

Michael came back to the office sweaty, frustrated and angry. He looked at the schedule. The stops were booked as they came in without any regard for efficient routing. When he asked Linda why she routed them that way, she barked back at him: "You try sitting here all day, with the phone ringing off the hook, with customers screaming at me, with you guys having problems on the road and me trying to coordinate solutions. Come on, Michael, I'm not sure how much more of this I can take."

"Linda, we've been at this for several years now, and look at us. What the heck are we doing wrong? There's money to be made here. I know there is. Look at how much money the big companies make. What are they doing differently?" "I don't know," Linda replied. "Let's go home. "Peter is coming home from school tonight; tomorrow is another day."

One of the most exciting parts of being a parent of a college student is when they come home for the summer. Peter just finished the coursework in his business program and was ready to work on his capstone project, which was the last thing he needed to do before earning his degree. He had a huge surprise for his mom and dad. His capstone was going to be an internship at Green Pest and Lawn Solutions. The internship was more like a consulting project, one in which he'd assess the business and act as a consultant to make recommendations to improve the business.

Peter loved his business program and was happy to be home. When the Halls arrived, Peter was unpacking and waiting for his mom and dad to come home and go out to dinner. After hugs and kisses, Michael, Linda and

Peter decided to go to the local burger joint for dinner. It was wonderful to have Peter home. He was talking excitedly about all the areas of business he studied. Michael explained the frustration they were experiencing with unhappy customers, operational, routing problems and the like. Michael liked the fact Peter decided to work in the family business and couldn't wait to get him started with his ongoing summer job. Well, Peter, let's get started tomorrow.

Dan's observations and recommendations

According to Albert Einstein, the definition of insanity is doing the same thing over and over and expecting a different result. Many business owners find themselves stuck in a rut because they use the same tactics every year and wonder why their businesses haven't improved. In this way, they've created their own little world of insanity.

While the business has grown in terms of revenue, the only reason it has is because Michael has heaped every aspect of the business on his shoulders. There have been no systems or processes to accomplish tasks and jobs. Everything was done based on the way Michael felt that day and the orders he gave. We see this approach to business all the time, and growth stagnates because the owner can't will his way to any more growth without managing a team to play the business game with a set of rules.

If this scenario sounds familiar, it's time to do something about it. It's up to you to put an end to the insanity. Do it for yourself and your business. Challenge yourself to do something different this year. Peel back the onion, and look at the different layers of your business.

It's frustrating when you're working hard on the battlefield, and it's difficult to stop to take a step back and look at your business as a whole. Who has the time and energy? But if you don't do something, you'll regret it. Remaining in the past is problematic. You're going to apply the same tactics and achieve the same results. Then you'll end up feeling the same way, which is depressing.

If this describes your situation, get out of this rut one way or another. If you don't, you'll be stuck in your own insanity, pacing in circles counting floor tiles in the cafeteria. Take another approach to change things up. Take action, and work your way out of the insanity.

If you see other businesses doing something different, try it. Get advice from professional coaches, business consultants, colleagues, or anyone else who might have new ideas.

Do research online, and read trade magazines. Listen to business improvement and motivational CDs. Attend training seminars and trade conferences. Do whatever it takes to implement new ideas into your business. But you don't have to overcomplicate things. Apply the K.I.S.S. method: Keep It Simple, Stupid! When keeping it simple, find a way to break the pattern. Do something different. You don't necessarily have to be radical, but try on a new hat. You want to have fresh ideas in your business, which is exciting.

New ideas expand the business and provide a framework of possibilities of where a business can progress and what the business can become. In many cases, new ideas come from outside a company. Be it consultants or peer groups, I've observed several second-generation young men and women come out of business school and start in the family business, growing it differently than their moms and dads did. These bright kids studied quantitative marketing, accounting, operations management, information technology, as well as organizational theory and design, in business school for four years. These young adults are taking the businesses that mom and dad elevated to a certain level by running as hard as they can, applying the principles they learned in school and working for larger organizations before entering the family business. That's where Peter hopes to make his mark on Green Pest and Lawn Solutions.

"The only thing worse than being incompetent, is not knowing you are."
—Anonymous

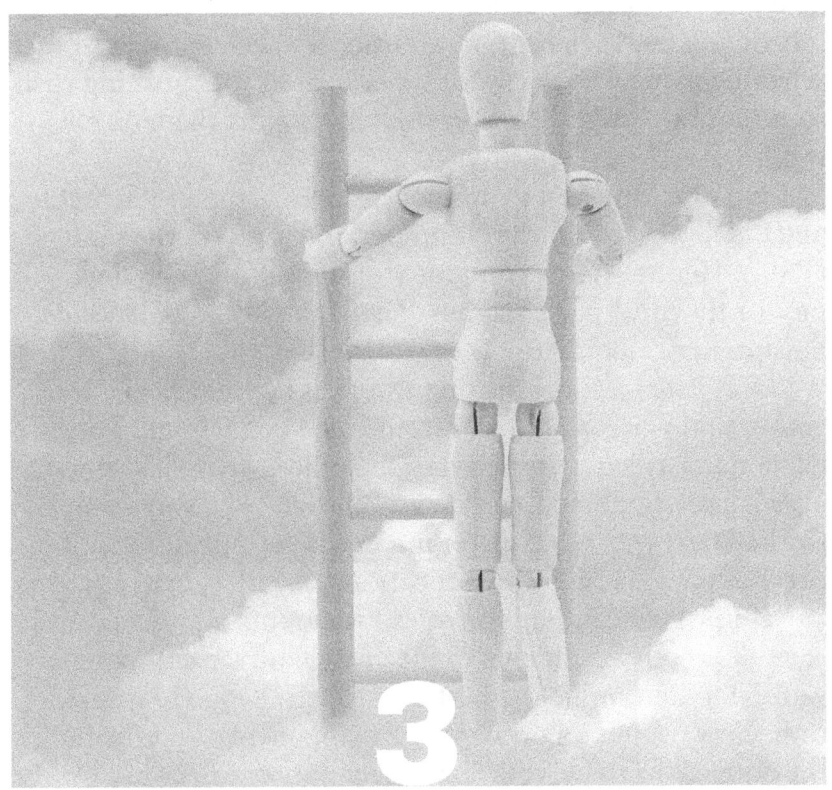

THE CORE OF YOUR BUSINESS:
What are you going to do,
and how will you do it?

"Peter, we've grown the business quite nicely since you went away to school. We've gotten rid of the answering service and purchased a voice-mail system, as well as a computer system we use to schedule work and record customer transactions," Michael said proudly as the two walked into the office the next morning.

Michael began his day like he does every day – by

listening to voice mail, calling back customers, and scheduling callbacks and new business. Michael tried to schedule all new business for himself after the morning rush so he could visit first-time customers to start them on the right foot.

Linda handles all the job tickets and customer payments and enters them into the computer and answers the phone all day. Her assistant, Jean, also answers phones all day; but for the most part, she puts people on hold while Linda finishes her call only to take the next one.

"OK, Peter. All the morning work is complete, so let's go out and work with the customers," Michael said. Peter, while not thrilled about leaving the office, where it seemed all business emanated, nodded to his dad. The two went to work. They were scheduled for a liquid termite application, two bee jobs and a lawn application.

Peter, while thinking the roles his parents had taken on weren't exactly conducive to the growth of the company, wanted to determine the best way to tell them. He wanted to begin working on growing the company, not performing the daily tasks that, while extremely important, could be handled by other well-trained employees.

At this point, he was riding in the truck with his dad, who he hadn't seen in a while. It was fantastic to catch up on their lives. Michael told Peter the nice thing about the first termite job was it was big money and would make most of his day. Additionally, the customer could pay an annual fee and extend the warranty. That seemed intriguing to Peter because the beauty of the business, in his opinion, was the recurring nature of the work.

"The next two jobs are bee jobs that will take us about a half hour each, and we'll make about a $150 bucks a pop," Michael said. "The lawn application will generate about $100, but it has been our biggest source of frustration because we handle lawn applications in rounds that usually are offset by 60 days. The problem is getting the future applications scheduled properly so each round is offset properly."

Peter was impressed with the termite business model, and while the lawn model seemed to need to be tweaked, what concerned him most were the bee jobs. He asked his dad, "When do we return for the second application? "Well, that's the beauty of the business," Michael said. "We only return if they call us within 30 days. After that, they're on their own, and we earn a lot of money for a small amount of work." "Why don't we try to put the bee jobs on a recurring cycle?" Peter asked. "Do you know how much work that would be to track?" Michael replied. "And besides, the customer called for bees. That's all they wanted."

Peter began to tell his dad about the four Ps of marketing he learned about in school:

1. Product (service)
2. Price
3. Promotion
4. Place

After discussing the four Ps of marketing, the two began understanding each other and their respective business philosophies.

Dan's observations and recommendations

The four Ps define what you're going to do in business and how you're going to do it. In the pest and lawn business, the first P is how you define your product. In this case, your service: What items are included, which ones aren't, what's the frequency, what materials are used, what expectations the customers should have when they ask for a callback, etc. We'll address the other three Ps in later chapters.

Many service-business owners think they're just providing one service. If this is the way you think, you're most likely leaving a chunk of money on the table so to speak. Developing tiered levels of packaged services provides your customers more choices and a higher level of service. The benefit and value to the client will be tremendous. Additionally, you don't have to peddle your services a la carte. Rather, you sell bundles of services to increase your revenue potential. Furthermore, you can attract more customers who have different needs, and you can provide the service for a lot less money. So, work toward developing your programs together.

While your onsite performing a service, you can add value to that service you're delivering by selling a package. It's cheap for you to deliver the additional service because you're already on the property; and the customer will come away with a higher perceived value because they're receiving complete coverage and peace of mind.

This is one of the most important secrets in this book!

You build wealth in the service industry by developing a book of service contracts. You're trying to increase the value of your company so someone who's interested in buying it can tell how valuable it is. If you want to sell your business, a purchaser will ask how much your recurring revenue is. Recurring revenue is commercial and residential route work- it's any service you provide regularly that provides a steady stream of revenue.

How much money will you make if you don't sell any new work? That answer will tell you the value of your company. Build the value of your company by building service contracts and renewable business you can count on year to year. This is called building an annuity base. So one day, when one of the big boys wants to buy you, you can say, "I generate $100,000 a month, and I don't do any advertising." If you can reach this point, your advertising initiatives become icing on the cake. That's how you can get more value from your business.

Defining your service programs

1. **What are your services?** List all of them on the left side of a sheet of paper.
2. **Identify which services are the bread and butter of your company.** Draw a circle around them. They'll be the basis of your service programs.
3. **Think of a number of program names**, and list them on the right side.
4. **Match services that can be grouped**, and draw a line between the service and program.
5. **Which services don't fit the service-program model** and should be considered as add-on services? Draw a square around these.

Developing your service programs is an ongoing process. Restructure your programs periodically to reinvent your service offerings and keep your relationships with your clients interesting. Apply this approach as a price-raising technique, too. You're not raising prices flat out. Instead, you're discontinuing an old program and replacing it with a new, more valuable, yet more expensive one that offers a higher level of service. If you were in the recurring service business, you could set up your programs like this:

- General pest control program
- General pest control and termite monitoring program
- The above including mosquito control
- The above including lawn care

Establish whatever program configurations you desire, but think about the customer and what each program includes. Why would they buy one program instead of another? Make sure there's value in each program and the value is communicated clearly. Also make sure the pricing tiers you establish make sense, and consider the cost of performing the service. Many service businesses go through a life cycle in which their marketability peaks and then fades. Try to restructure your plans as certain services start to phase out.

Communicating an entire program

You have a new program and are raising prices and generating more income. You're also delivering more value to your clients. Now you have to get the word out. Identify what differentiates you from your competition, and determine what your unique selling proposition is. Develop a process through which you'll make adjustments to your program structure.

Converting your clients to service programs can be a touchy topic. Contact all your clients via telephone or mail to make sure you communicate the benefits and value of the new programs clearly and accurately. Be careful because you don't want to send mixed messages.

For example, offer a home protection plan. Not all clients will want to include all services in their plan. A pool service might offer a total service that includes opening, closing and chemical maintenance; however, some might want to apply their own chemicals, so offer a complete service or one with only the components. This way the customer knows what he'll pay for the season, and you'll know what your revenue stream looks like.

Create programs that offer peace of mind for service continuity. You're putting an end to your client's sleepless nights. Be results-oriented, and earn the trust of your customers by delivering high-quality services that are professional and effective. Remember, a worrisome public is your target market, and peace of mind is your product offering.

You're trying to sell your customers an entire program

and have them sign on for an all-inclusive standard plan. Most customers are interested in only one or a few services, but by packaging a plan and stacking one service on another, the perceived value is much higher, and you can generate considerably more money for it.

Marketing services

Most services are intangible and can't be packaged or put on a shelf. The customer can't hold or touch it. So, here's the most effective approach to marketing your company's services: Sell them based on perceived value and the end result you offer. Focus your marketing efforts on the results of the delivered service. If you can convince your prospective client that you can ease their worries, then you're on your way to making the sale. You might think you're offering a service, but you're really offering something much more important and extremely valuable – peace of mind. Do what you're good at. Set up a service program based on your company's core competencies. Spend most of your time playing the games you're good at so you're better positioned to dominate them.

Stick to your core competencies

If you have a popular service program that's taking off, promote that service more, and set up your business to deliver that service profitably and efficiently. You want to be the king of that type of service program and rule that market space.

Look at Michael Jordan's basketball career with the Chicago Bulls. You couldn't have asked for more in terms of skill and accomplishment. Now contrast that with Michael Jordan's attempt to play professional baseball with the Chicago White Sox minor league team. It was a dismal failure, and he never even made it to the Major Leagues. It turns out that, despite his incredible athletic ability, playing baseball wasn't one of Jordan's core competencies.

Build your business around your programs

When developing your business, stay program-centric. The thought process is:

- **Your wealth completely or partly depends on your business' value.**
- **Your business' value is based on how much renewable work you perform annually.**
- **Your renewable work depends on how many service contracts you've sold.**

So, convert your clients to your program-centric model of service agreements because it's a key part of your business' success and will be critical to your ability to build wealth.

It's fine to sell add-on services, but be careful not to dilute your company's core image or presentation. To offer add-ons, you'll need to develop additional competencies within your business. Be clear about what you're offering your clients.

*"We will never try to develop a strategy that wins on price.
There is nothing unique about pricing."*

—*Josh S. Weston*

PRICING

Michael's day went quicker than usual because he had
Peter trench and drill holes while he pumped termiticide and
patched them. The bee jobs and the lawn stops went much
quicker with Peter's help. Michael enjoyed having Peter
help progress the work more quickly. The conversation was
terrific -- Michael was teaching Peter the techniques used
to finish the tasks needed to complete the services sold, and
Peter spoke to Michael about the concepts he learned in his
business program.

Peter was thinking about a case study relating to the airline industry he analyzed during his last semester. People who have advanced degrees in business and vast experience in operating businesses run U.S. airlines. The class discussion revolved around the fact that, almost weekly, prices in the industry change, doubling one week and falling by half the next. The professor presented the case for the airlines. He explained the pricing strategy: Once airline schedules are set, almost all costs are fixed, so the pricing strategy was all about filling the seats in the airplanes. If they could fill the flights with higher-priced tickets, the flight would be profitable. If prices were too low, even filling the flight with lower-priced fares would result in a loss for that flight. However, because the costs were committed (i.e., the schedules were set, and the planes were going to travel no matter how many people were flying), it was all about filling the planes. If there was even one passenger, his fare would reduce the potential loss of the costs committed to making the trip. Each incremental passenger would reduce the loss until there were enough passengers to cover the cost, and once breakeven was achieved, each passenger fare would be sheer profit (at least adding to gross margin).

Why would anyone want a business model like this?

Peter asked his dad, "Do you ever take jobs just to keep everyone busy, even if it was a losing job?" Michael said, "Of course." Peter thought for a minute and continued, "But dad, this is a strategy that's a one-way ticket to bankruptcy court. One day, our prices are high, maybe getting some jobs; and the next day, they're low just to keep everyone busy. Besides not pricing consistently, we train our customers to believe they'll pay less solely by waiting until we're slower. On the surface, it's not a bad strategy, but soon it will lead to lower pricing across the board. At some point, our cost structure and desired profit need to be figured into our pricing, or else we'll be working for free or worse, losing money on the work we perform." "I see your point Peter, but what do you suggest?" Michael said.

"Well, remember the four Ps of marketing?" Peter said. "We spoke about the first P and designing the product (or in our case the service). The second P is pricing. So dad, how do you arrive at the prices you charge for each of your services?"

Michael began, "When you've been doing this a while, you develop a sense of what people are willing to pay and what the competition is charging, so you charge a little less than what the competition charges." Michael continued, "If everyone else is charging that price and making money that should be good enough for us."

"I guess it should," Peter answered. "But the way I see it, we should understand our direct and indirect costs as a percentage of revenue. We learned this effective technique for pricing called Break-even Analysis (BEA) in my accounting and finance classes.

Dan's observations and recommendations

The four Ps define what you're going to do in business and how you're going to do it. In the pest and lawn business, the first P is how you define a product or service. The second P is pricing, which is important because it's one of the most powerful ways a company can improve its performance. How effective is your pricing policy?

Three examples:
- An effective pricing policy will keep you profitable and successful.
- A mediocre pricing policy will keep you frustrated and barely in business, wondering what needs to be done to succeed.
- An ineffective pricing policy will put you out of business.

When determining what to charge, consider:
- What the market will bare
- Fixed costs
- Variable costs
- What your best competitor charges

Staying successful by employing an effective pricing policy means increasing profit, beating the competition and creating wealth. Price increases or decreases have a magnification effect on profit. The reason is simple: Price increases usually reach the bottom line in one piece, while the advantages of lower unit costs or higher sales are diluted. Once breakeven is achieved, price increase is extremely powerful and impacts the bottom line significantly. Thus, for a company with 10-percent margins, a 10-percent price increase could produce a 100-percent increase of profit to 20 percent. This works the other way as well: A 10-percent decrease of price decreases profit 100 percent, taking a 10-percent margin to zero margin or breakeven. Let's look at an example.

If revenue plus cost structure per hour is:

Sales	**$ 70.00**
Direct labor	$ 17.00
Chemicals	$ 6.00
Vehicle	$ 8.00
Other direct	$ 4.00
Selling advertising	$ 10.00
General & admin.	$ 18.00
Total cost	**$ 63.00**
	======
Profit	**$ 7.00**
	======

If we change the sales price to $77.00, we doubled the profit by 100 percent to $14.00 because there are no additional costs associated with providing this service. This is a double-edged sword because reducing your price by $3.50 will cut your profit by half. A reduction of $7.00 will wipe out your entire profit. Again, be careful in this regard because you need to know what effect price changes will have on your bottom line.

Raising prices - it's easy, so just do it

Of course, there's a potential problem when raising prices because when prices increase, the number of buyers tend to decrease. This is why pricing has always been viewed as a delicate art of finding the balance between the two. Nevertheless, larger profits would be possible if more companies treated pricing and price increases as a task to be performed at least annually using a quantitative model considering time and overhead. So, now you might be asking yourself, "What should my prices be?" Before you change prices, clarify what type of pricing policy fits your business model and positioning compared to others in your local market and how you want your company viewed by the public. You need pricing perspective. Do you want to be a low-price provider, or would you rather sell a premium service? There might be sound reasons for being a low-price seller, just not as a small operator in the pest control or lawn care businesses.

Michael Dell started as a low-cost operator and became successful, although the Dell brand isn't the lowest-price brand anymore. Costco and Amazon are two other examples. If you look to these models for inspiration being the low-cost business in the market, you must have a firm grasp on:

- Margins
- Deep pockets
- The ability to do big volume

Without these three, you'll go broke. Most small businesses don't have these resources, so don't commit business suicide. Don't be a low-baller.

What will attract the type of customers you want? Your price is a strong signal to your potential clients telling them who you are in the marketplace. If your goal is to raise the quality of your clientele, the easiest way to do that is increase your prices.

I like high-volume accounts. I'm not saying be a lower-price operator. I'm saying have many accounts that don't take long to service. The price per hour is high. It's alright to have a few accounts that take hours or full days to complete the service, but if you build a business full of these accounts, you'll always be at their beck and call because they figure they're the big fish and can monopolize your time with every little problem. You'll soon realize your business can only grow so big. By the same token, if you build a business full of these large accounts, you'll have to hire expensive management to run them, or you'll need to run them yourself. In this scenario, you can make a comfortable income, but you won't build wealth (value of your company) because you'll be the go-to guy for every issue with the larger clients.

Do you want a high-volume transactional business, or would you rather develop long-term, nurturing client relationships? If you want to build something easy to scale and perhaps sell down the road, high volume, low touch might fit the bill. If you're developing a life style business to carry you into old age or a business with a strong public image, think long term and nurturing. Either way, your price per hour needs to be high enough to make a reasonable profit.

Develop a pricing perspective that fits your goals. Your decision will go a long way to determine whom you do business with and how you do it, as well as how you can harvest your business. There are no clear guidelines to map the right choice. It's more a matter of preference and positioning. Let's review the three types of pricing strategies you can employ:

1. **Price to time.** This is what most service people do. They set their prices by the hour or day. The biggest problem is this makes it too easy for prospects to compare your price. It also puts them in control of your time if they do buy.
2. **Price to competition.** This is the most common form of pricing and is the core of all prices based on market research. It makes sense if your offer is comparable to that of your competitors, and they're profitable.
3. **Front-end or loss-leader pricing.** Loss-leader pricing isn't designed to generate operating profits. Its purpose is to take market share from competitors or create customers to whom you'll later sell other products and services. Remember, it's difficult to raise prices after you've gone in too low.

If your goal is to drive your competitors out of business, and you have deep pockets to sustain an unprofitable price war, this can work brilliantly. Many big box retailers, including Staples and Home Depot, have followed this strategy. Many years of low prices eventually crushed their competitors, and both raised prices when their markets thinned out.

No matter what your strategy is, pricing is your supersonic weapon – one that if understood properly will make you wealthy or make you feel that if only you had one more sale you could pay your bills or worse than that will drive you into insolvency. The choice is yours. Harness the power of the pricing weapon, or fail.

Keep your prices up
If you view your service as a commodity, you give away

your ability to differentiate your product and receive the price you deserve. This is why you need to understand the features and benefits of your service and understand why your service is different, why those differences are important to the customer, and how to effectively communicate that to the customer. If you can't tell why you're better than the guy down the street, you may as well close up shop and work for him. Your customer will pay a premium price if you're better to do business with. Ponder the following questions:

- Do you provide better service?
- Do you pay more attention to customers' needs?
- Are your technicians better trained?
- Do you offer quicker response times?
- Are the people answering your phones knowledgeable?
- Do they have a can-do attitude?
- Is it easy to have someone call your customers back when there's a problem?
- Do you offer a 100-percent satisfaction guarantee?
- Is your service time flexible?
- Do you provide a newsletter that gives pest and lawn tips?
- Do you offer multiple methods for customers to pay (i.e., credit card, check, cash, Automated Clearing House)?
- Do you offer payment terms?
- Are you an admirable corporate citizen who donates time and money to local charities?

These are things that can make you better than your competitor and help you justify higher prices. In fact, customers will pay a higher price for a service and even pay the same company a higher price for the same item. Examples include light service; guaranteed, two-hour callback service; and nonchemical treatments.

The reality is customers don't buy based solely on price. They often think they do; but if they did, everyone would be driving a Yugo (remember Yugos?). They almost always tell you they do. Many times price is the only thing they have to compare because they don't understand what we do. Sometimes they use different tactics to convince us to reduce our prices. They give you the old, "We can only pay so much money," or "We can't pay any more than $75 per month for this service. When this happens, respond with this: "How did you come up with that price?" That's when they say:

- "Because that's what my husband said."
- "Because that's what my boss said."
- "Because that's what the facilities guys said."

In effect, they're identifying the people who make the decisions to buy your service. Now you know the decision maker, so pursue him.

"I can receive the same service from the guy down the street, only cheaper." When a customer tells you this, the first thing you need to think about is can he receive the same service? Services aren't always the same. They're often just similar. For example, he wants to be serviced on Tuesday at 10:00 p.m. Your competitors will service him only during normal working hours – not the same.

The next thing a customer will say is, "It doesn't make any difference. I don't care what time the service is." He'll try to negate your difference. But often, it makes a difference, and a savvy sales technique will help point out why. Frequently, minor differences are significant ones, especially when it comes to the service you provide.

But what if you have the same service, or the minor difference isn't important? Your customer might say, "You're just selling a commodity. You're selling pest or lawn service, and it is what it is. One guy is just like another guy. Everything is identical, and I can get it cheaper from your competitor."

How should you react to this? Agree it's pest or lawn service, but that doesn't mean it's the same deal. Even when your competitor has the same service, your customer might well prefer to buy it from you because you're easier to do business with, you're close by, your billing procedures are better, you have better operating hours, your people are friendlier and better trained, you have same-day emergency service or whatever.

When a customer tells you, "I can get the same service down the street, only cheaper," he might be able to get the same service, but he's not going to be buying it from the same company. Your customer is telling you, "I want that guy's price, but I want the way you do business."

"Your prices are too high." When someone tells you this, your reaction should be, "Well, of course we're higher than anybody else, and I'm very proud of that. Let me tell you why." When you openly acknowledge your prices are higher than others, you set yourself up for giving an excellent presentation because you're admitting your prices are higher and your customers want to know why? Price makes a statement. Now you get to show off your service and sell them.

No matter how hard customers hammer you on price, don't be squeamish about being firm. Furthermore, don't be afraid to raise prices when warranted. You're not going to lose all your sales when you raise your prices. If price were the only reason anybody bought anything, only one company would be selling all that's sold. Think about this: If you lost all your sales by raising your price, then how has anyone raised prices during the past 100 years?

It's all about selling time. You're a professional, and you sell time. Woody Allen once said 90 percent of life is showing up. I'd add that for the successful service company owner, not only is it showing up, but it's also charging the customer for the time you're there.

What has always attracted me to the service industry is its simplicity. Running a pest or lawn business isn't easy, but the business model is simple. Lawyers and accountants charge by the hour. What about you? Consider these examples:

1. **The chiropractor.** You hurt your back. You visit a chiropractor. He puts you through an initial procedure for which he charges you and has you return weekly or monthly for maintenance.
2. **The accountant.** You hire an accountant. He looks at your past tax returns and your books and records from the past, for which he charges you for, and has you return monthly to complete your accounting.
3. **The pool maintenance man.** In the spring, he opens your pool. He adds chemicals all season. In the fall, he closes your pool.

It's obvious how these examples parallel what you do. It's all about selling time. The successful pest and lawn care operator understands he must become competent at the skills needed to eliminate pests and green up lawns. In fact, the more you can standardize the procedures and add value for customers the greater return per hour.

Remember, selling time is somewhat intangible, but the results of what we do aren't (i.e., eliminating pests, making a lawn look beautiful). Customers can't come to a store and look at, touch or feel what you do, which creates challenges and is unique to the service industry. To reduce intangibility, buyers look for signals of service quality to be assured they're not making a mistake. Some companies deal with this by offering service guarantees. Response time might be one of these or money back if a customer isn't satisfied.

The amount of money you charge a customer usually is predicated on the time it takes to perform the service. As mentioned above, you're essentially selling time, which is a perishable commodity. Once it's gone, it can't be resold.

Think about a fruit stand. The owner can sell fresh fruit all day for a sizable profit. Once the fruit rots, it can't be sold. The same is true with time. If your technician is spending time doing anything other than servicing a customer, you can never have the time back, and it can never be resold because it's unsellable. Not only can't you sell time in the past, but it also has a cost. Even if a technician is paid on percentage of production, there's still a cost to unproductive time (i.e., the cost of the truck and idle equipment and the opportunity cost of not having him on the job).

If your routing is efficient, you'll be able to maximize the amount of time you can sell. If it's not, you'll always be asking yourself why you're making so little money. Your time is what you sell. If you offer quality time (i.e., competent service and flexible customer service) at an acceptable return per hour, and you schedule it efficiently, you're sure to make a healthy profit, maximizing the value of your company, thereby building wealth.

To price your time, understand your cost structure for you to price your services for profit. The following focuses on the accurate cost of doing business and choosing prices accordingly. The service-pricing model is based on two variables – time and money (hourly rate).

Time. The service time is how long it takes to fulfill the obligation of eliminating a customer's pest problem or greening their lawn under the service program. This includes treatment and callback time. The benefit of being an experienced service professional is you can reasonably estimate the time it takes to complete the job, as well as callback time, for the average customer. Service professionals who earn the most money realize that while they provide pest and lawn services, what they're really selling is time (to effectively service their customer). Material costs are involved, but because the service you perform is consistent, you can build the material costs into the model. Every action that makes more efficient use of time will provide larger profits. This isn't to say you must trade quality workmanship for time; rather, you must make reasonable estimates of the time it takes to provide quality service.

Money. This is an hourly charge for your service that covers your costs and allows you to make a reasonable profit. How do you know what that hourly rate should be? Accountants calculate this number using a technique called break-even analysis.

Break-even analysis

The following will give you a basis to determine your hourly rate. Think hard about the following discussion because your profitability relies on it. Remember, service is your profession; therefore, you should never sell yourself cheap. After all, you're providing a needed service, and if it's communicated to the customer that way, you'll be able to command your price. And you deserve it.

Fixed costs are those that remain constant at any volume of business (i.e., rent, advertising, utilities).

Variable costs are those associated with producing one unit of a good or service. For this purposes, one unit of a service equates to one hour of service. Thus, variable costs are those that rise and fall based on the number of hours you provide service. Examples of variable costs are hourly pay for employees, workers compensation insurance and material costs.

Gross profit is the difference between the price charged per unit (hour of service) and the variable costs. For example, if you bill your service at $100 per hour and a technician earns $20 an hour and all other variable costs associated with providing that hour of service are $35, your gross profit would be $45 (figured: $100 billed less $55 variable costs).

Once you understand these definitions clearly, you can

determine your break-even point, which in units (service hours) equals fixed costs divided by gross profit per hour.

Example: If your rent, utilities and all other fixed costs are $10,000 and your using the example above, your gross profit is $45 an hour, and your break-even point is $222.2 hours of service at $100 an hour just to break even ($10,000 divided by $45 gross profit per hour). At 222.2 hours of service, you'll start making a profit of $45 per hour. Gross profit contributes to paying the fixed costs. Once the fixed costs are paid, the gross profit contributes to bottom-line profit, which is the reason some accountants call gross profit the contribution margin.

Is it really this simple? Yes. However, at various sales levels, certain fixed costs rise, such as after a certain sales level, a new piece of equipment might have to be added, so the cost of using that piece of equipment must be added to fixed costs. So figuring your break-even point can be confusing sometimes.

The aforementioned explanation is accurate in terms of pricing methodology. Some would argue a small operator could operate at lower prices because he doesn't have the overhead the larger companies do. There's nothing further from the truth because the costs might vary slightly from company to company. But over the long run, the cost structure is the same for the small and large operator alike.

A single-person operation has the same cost structure as larger companies. However, a small guy can be his own technician, run his own books and perform all the office functions himself. (This is the way a small guy should operate.) In this manner, you might think you're saving all that money in technician and office salaries, and the savings is going right to your bottom line, making you much more profitable.

The problem with this line of thought is you're in business to make a profit and, perhaps, build a valuable business that you might sell someday. You can get a job as a technician and a job as an office worker at night. Working these jobs would pay you a fair wage.

Why would you take all the risks associated with going into business if your plan didn't include making more money than a wage earner? The profit is your reward for taking the risk. If you operate under the false illusion that you can cut your price because your costs are lower, you'll eliminate this reward for taking the risk. You might not only wipe out your profit, you might even cut into the wage portion. (It might still appear you're making money because there's some wage left, not all.)

At this point, why be in business for yourself? You can earn more money working for someone else doing the same amount of work. So you beat the competition by providing quality service, not necessarily lower price.

"Doing business without marketing is like winking at a girl in the dark. You know what you are doing, but nobody else does."

—*Stuart Henderson*

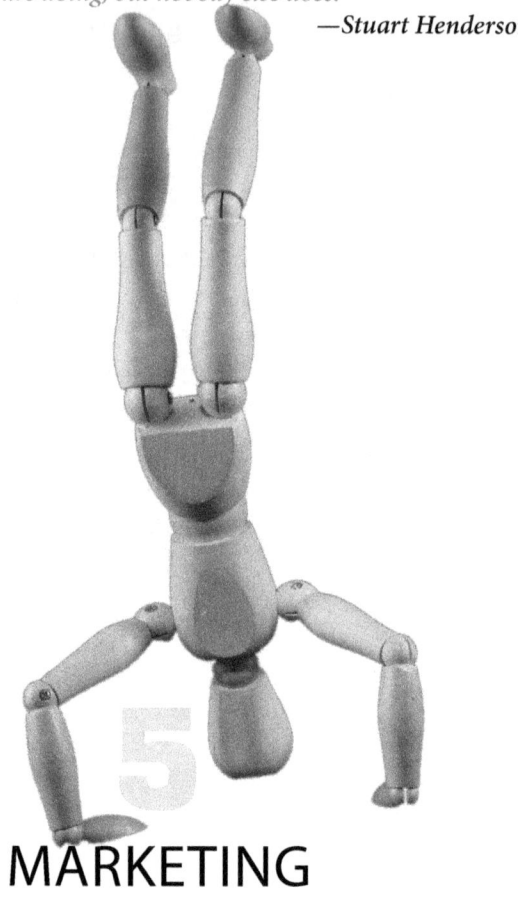

MARKETING

Michael enjoyed having Peter around. It was fun to see his son voice opinions that made sense. It also was worthwhile to have his son shadow him all day, learning the daily trials and tribulations a business owner experiences.

"Peter, tomorrow I have my Yellow Page representative coming in to talk about our advertising program," Michael said. "Great dad – what percentage of your advertising dollars do you spend with him?" Peter asked. "Almost all of it," Michael replied. "Does it work?" Peter asked. "Not like it used to," Michael answered. "The Yellow Pages used to be like a license to print money. But we don't seem to generate the volume from it we used to." Peter followed up the question by asking his dad how much he's spending and how he's tracking the amount of sales derived from the Yellow Pages. Michael replied he wasn't sure how much he was paying. "Basically, I speak to my rep, and he tells me what the spend will be for the year, and I agree or disagree. Tracking would be difficult and probably not worth the effort. Peter, when you've been in the business a long time, you have to trust your gut because it usually tells you what to do."

"Hey dad, we spoke about product and price, the first two Ps," Peter said. "The third P is promotion and has to do with a mix of advertising campaigns, the positioning of our service in the market place and the expected return of the campaigns. I'd love to carve out quiet time where you and I work out an advertising plan, from the message we're sending to our prospective and current customers and how much we're willing to spend to bring in those customers. Can we do that?" "Yes, Peter. Let's sit down this weekend and do that. I'm looking forward to it."

Saturday morning arrived, and just as they had agreed, Peter and Michael sat down to discuss how marketing decisions are made.

Michael explained the company's marketing revolves around the Yellow Pages and direct mail. Peter asked how that decision was made? "Because that's what everyone else does, and it seems to work," Michael replied. Peter asked how he knew it worked, and Michael said because we have all of this work. Peter asked how much of the work is a direct result of the money spent this year versus customers they worked for in the past who keep using their services. "In other words dad, do we have a way to measure how successful we are?" Peter asked. "Are those two methods of advertising working because the world is changing? There are fewer people depending on those mediums because more people are relying on the Internet for information."

Dan's observations and recommendations

Where do you start promoting your business? First, identify and define your unique selling proposition (USP) – it's what makes your business better than anyone else's. If a potential client asks you, "Why should I use your services instead of another company's services?" your USP is the answer; and hopefully, if it's good enough, it becomes their answer, too.

Have you ever tried to sell your programs to a potential client only to hear them say, "Oh, you're just like the other guy"? They may say you use the same materials and do the same work using the same techniques, which can be frustrating.

In this business, it's easy for customers to commoditize your services. Well, if you have a convincing USP, it makes it difficult for customers to commoditize the services you offer because you don't offer the same general service everyone else does. You have more value to offer your clients.

Now you have to determine what that is. Learn how to create distance and separation between you and the next guy. Pull away from the crowd. Your USP is an important component of your marketing program. In every different market in which you compete, you can advertise a different USP.

Differentiate yourself in many ways. Communicate several USPs to your market throughout your advertising and the fabric of your company. Keep in mind you can't be everything to everyone.

Develop your business-marketing plan. For so many business owners, marketing is an afterthought, but it needs to be a core function of your business. To sell services to your market successfully, be proactive and plan ahead.

Create a marketing plan that maps out your specific short- and long-term marketing activities. Include a budget for your advertising, and know exactly how much you spent on each marketing activity so you can calculate your return on investment later. When developing your marketing plan, consider the following:

• **Identify your USP.** When you develop your marketing plan, think of your USP and how you can pitch it to the market. Can you verbalize your USP?
• **Define your target market.** Where's your hungry market? Conduct market research to locate the pain points of a hungry market, and set your sights on it.
• **Know your competition.** Know who else is in the market with you. Understand how big your competition is and their USP. Identify how you'll compete.
• **Align your sales cycles with your promotional plan.** You know when the sales season hits your business-when you have a captive audience. Plan your marketing efforts to coincide with this time as best you can. Always remember the timing of your marketing is essential to its effectiveness and success.

The service business is need based, so timing plays a large role in how you roll out your marketing initiatives. In marketing, the decision-making unit (DMU) is the one who holds the power of decision making. This can be a homeowner, contractor or building manager. The trick is to forecast when the DMU will be at a decision-making point, which can be difficult to determine. Think about the DMU and what his main interest is, what keeps him busy and when he has time to listen to your pitch. If you can time the delivery of your message so it hits at the exact time, your marketing activities will succeed .

In the service industry, most of your advertising activities will take place during the seasonal peak. Deliver multiple hits to the customer in a short period of time, which can be extremely powerful. The main idea is to fish in the pond where the fish are. Some say your name should be out there constantly. That's true, but it's important your name be out there much more during the seasonal peaks.

A few words about branding

Companies such as GE or IBM are able to spend millions of dollars building a brand. But you and I don't have the money to do this; therefore, the best area to spend your marketing dollars is on direct-response marketing. On the other hand, there are basic areas where small-budget brand building is a must.

You need a logo people identify with and relate to. Once your logo and slogan are crafted, determine where you're going to put it. Appropriate places are business cards, brochures, paperwork, signage and uniforms. On such items, make sure you represent your business in a consistent manner so your customers don't become confused. Most, if not all, small businesses don't have the marketing budget to build a brand the way huge corporations do. Small-time branding on your stationary, signs and uniforms is about as close to building a brand in your customers' eyes as you'll get; but don't worry, this will be enough.

Don't waste your money on small-business branding. So many small-business owners pour dollar after dollar into big-time branding. Well, that doesn't work, and it's a waste of money. For example, sponsoring a sign at a charity golf outing is a waste of money if all you get is a sign with your logo on it by the tee. Don't get me wrong, you might be donating money to a good cause, which is a great thing to do, but this isn't a marketing initiative that's going to give you a return on your investment. If you want to make such a marketing initiative successful, be on the course shaking hands with golfers, greeting them when they walk by your sign and handing out promotions and giveaways. But be smart with your advertising dollars, because if you're a small service company, you don't have much money to throw away on a lonesome sign by a golf tee.

Build your street credibility. Services are a relationship business; therefore, you and your employees need to meet and impress people with your company. Credibility goes a long way in small business, and it's no different for service professionals. Consistent delivery of high-quality services is the straightest path to building credibility. Stay focused on quality, and your credibility will take care of itself.

If you don't use brand building, then use direct response marketing, and you'll develop a cache of credibility in your region and inevitably develop a brand throughout time.

Identifying your business' target market is critical. Know who your clients are, and understand what market they're in. Determine what market your clients are in and which market you want your future clients to come from. Services are a relationship business, and it's common that a homeowner who has lived in a house for 10 years has developed a relationship with a friend of the family, friend of a friend or perhaps just another business.

It can be difficult to break into markets where other service companies are already working and forging their own customer relationships. Sometimes you have to overcome a perception of value and an expectation around price. Yet, new homeowners can be a valuable source for new customers. Usually, they don't have regular home services. That's why so many service companies like to market to new home buyers; and this approach can be successful if executed correctly.

So what's your target market? The following are examples of successfully profitable areas:

- couples 30 to 50 years old with young children who

just bought a new home;
* property management companies;
* country clubs; and
* warehousing businesses.

Make sure you know who your clients are and what type of service you're offering and how they fit together. Understand what kind of customer you're looking for and split the customer base into categories.

Break it down any way you want, but think about who your customer is, then think about who you want your customer to be, and then mail or email something to that customer.

Test, execute and monitor your marketing efforts

"Ready, aim, fire!" is much better than "Ready, fire, aim!" In marketing, the approach is similar. Rather than blowing all your money on unproven marketing tactics that deliver poor results, you're better off testing several approaches. To test how effective your marketing is, you need to determine how you'll track the results, which will help you to identify which tactics provide the highest return on your marketing investment, minimizing your losses and maximizing your gains.

Make sure you have a solid system and you're disciplined. It's about timing, the message you're sending and the venue to which you sent your message. But how do you know what works? We say this all the time: "If you can't measure it, you can't manage it!" You have to build the ability to measure return on investment into the fabric of your business. You need to measure your results constantly to see what works best and make adjustments as you move forward. Whether you're using a computer system to track incoming calls or merely keeping an ongoing tally on a paper pad, make sure you capture this information somewhere.

Receive a phone call from a new customer? Ask your

customers how they heard about you. Offer coupons with promotion codes your customers will give you to get their discount. This will tell you which marketing initiative worked on a particular customer. Capture as much information as possible from cable, radio, newspapers, or any marketing technique. Whatever method you use, make your best attempt to capture as much information about a lead and how they reached you.

Today's marketing arena is crowded, which is all the more reason to track and measure marketing to see what works best. One more thing, take action based on your results. So many people are afraid to abort a marketing campaign because they already spent money on it. Well, consider it a sunk cost, get back whatever money you can and move on.

Coupons

Use coupons to entice customers and track marketing. Offering discounts through coupons can be an effective way to entice new customers to use your services. Coupons can be sent in the mail through Val-Pak and Money Mailer, as well as email campaigns. In addition to enticing customers, coupons can help you track your marketing's effectiveness.

Promotional marketing is an approach to marketing that stimulates a prospective buyer to take action through several incentives. The most common and effective is coupons. There are a number of ways to track and measure the results. The easiest way to measure the effectiveness of coupon marketing is to have the customer send the coupons back to you. Examples of coupons in action include:

- offering a discount or promotional rate;
- having the current customer refer a friend;
- offering inactive customers a discount
  to renew their service in the off-season; and
- offering a free gift for responding.

This interaction, dialogue, regular communication, measured response ... this is what you want. This is what will make marketing more effective. So, measure the effectiveness of your coupons to see which offer works best. What motivates the customer? It's all in the offer you present.

It all ties to permission marketing and developing and taking this client from a stranger, to a friend, to a client and finally to a great client.

Direct mail

Direct mail, which offers a significant return on investment, is a great way to advertise because you're sending specific and targeted messages to your mailing list. Delivering the right message in the right market is likely to provide a significant return on investment. The most difficult part of direct mail campaigns is getting your hands on a good list. Direct mail can be enormously successful, and the return on investment can be tremendous. Just make sure you have the right approach so you don't end up wasting money. Techniques that will help you improve the success rate of your direct mail campaigns are:

- Make it short and sweet!
- Align your message with your target market.
- Be specific and clear in your offer and the benefit to your client.
- Avoid big words and write at an elementary school level.
- Write copy with a personal and conversational tone.
- Provide a guarantee or no-risk offer.
- Give the customer a deadline to take action.
- Provide testimonials from current customers.
- Call to action.

P.S. Use the postscript to grab their attention one last time.

Telemarketing

Telemarketing isn't for the faint of heart. It takes resources, time and perseverance. To implement a telemarketing campaign, make sure training is thorough and the script is dummy-proof, with question-and-answer responses from which reps can read. It's important you have well-thought-out scripting. Even if the telemarketer doesn't use the script word-for-word, they should use the general framework to be effective. Use powerful words when calling customers. Residential cold calling has become more difficult because of the recent do-not-call laws, but cold calling to commercial targets can be effective. If a customer is already yours, telemarketing added services usually provide a worthwhile return on investment.

Telemarketing is one of the most ugly, successful marketing techniques that works. So, it costs about $4 per hour to be on the phone on local calls. Let's say you pay someone $12 an hour to make those calls. Add overhead, and you're looking at about $20 per hour for your telemarketing endeavor.

Let's say the average lead from a mailer, e-mailer or the Yellow Pages costs between $100 and $500. That would give you about five to 25 hours to make one sale to equal other successful methods. Here's why it's ugly: Have you ever watched how many times someone gets hung up on during 10 hours of telemarketing? Trust me, it's ugly. But if you make just one sale, you're doing just as good as your other marketing mediums. If you close two sales you're doing better. So, although telemarketing is ugly and it's difficult to watch, it's extremely cost effective. Remember to respect your-do-not call list.

Finally, when you tell a sales lead you'll call him back,

make sure you have a method to follow up and make good on your promise. Keep detailed records of your calls using a contact management program to ensure you don't forget to call your new friend.

Create a system to ask for testimonials and then brag about them. If you don't get into the knack of asking your clients for testimonials, you're unlikely to receive them. Develop a system for collecting testimonials. After all, who best to brag about your company's services than your clients?

When you receive testimonials, file them. Create a brag book of what current clients say about your business and share that with other customers. Use this as a resource for accolades to be called on whenever you need it. Put them on your website, but make sure you get permission from the endorser. Also, incorporate testimonials into your banners and posters. Create flyers with testimonials to give to customers.

There are many different ways you can use a testimonial to your advantage. It's an ideal marketing tool. It's an even better sales exhibit. It's an inspirational motivator for your workforce. It also can be a motivator for you.

Now that you see the value and the power of a testimonial, the more difficult part is collecting them. Establish a system for collecting testimonials, and make sure receipts are delivered with forms so customers can use to submit testimonials. When your CSRs resolve an issue for a customer, make sure part of the telephone script includes a request for a testimonial. When technicians perform a service, make sure they ask for testimonials when they're on site. Technicians can give the customer a testimonial form, which can be filled out while a technician is on site performing a service.

OK, so where's the incentive to spend time filling out a testimonial form? Create an incentive for the customers as well as your employees. Make a contest out of it. Create a best testimonial contest with a free giveaway, or offer a discount for submitting a testimonial. Additionally, motivate your staff by offering a prize to the employee who collects the most testimonials.

How about social media? When you hear the term social media, what does it mean to you? If you're like most service businesses, it means the new frontier in marketing. With the rise and fall of the Yellow Pages as the most important advertising outlet in our industry, service professionals are struggling to find cost-effective ways to secure new business. For many, social media is a way forward.

The beauty of social media is that it's not just a marketing tool, and if the business owner is able to embrace the entire concept of social media, he'll discover it can be used to improve many areas of business. While many believe setting up a profile on Facebook or LinkedIn, or creating a Twitter account and participating or monitoring conversations, is a social media strategy, this is only the first step.

Social media is about determining what outcome you want, quantifying that outcome and building a network that will help you achieve those objectives, which can be sales dollars, as well as technical learning such as technician training, learning business-building concepts such as running a more efficient operation, improving your accounting or personnel management, or sharing business experiences and strategies with others in the industry.

Your initial social media strategy could be to simply improve communication within your company. In this case, your network might be all the employees in your company. Having each employee posting and commenting about what they're working on, new policies and procedures, or how to deal with customer problems that seem to repeat themselves provides a terrific team-building tool. A word of caution in this area though – you need to have guidelines about the amount of time spent on social media and permissible content because Facebook and LinkedIn can become time consuming and unproductive, as well as negative if you let it go unchecked.

From a marketing prospective, assume you wanted to focus your sales effort on local property managers. A relevant network to build might be a property manager group for the region you serve. If this is the route you're going to take, be careful not to make it exclusively about pest control or lawn care because this topic could be too narrow for the group. Your sales efforts should address as many problems these folks deal with as possible. In this manner, your sales effort gives them a reason to visit the group more often. Once there, you can start conversations about pest control or lawn care, which makes you the expert when these issues arise and a property manager needs advice.

Remember, social media is about conversations, not hard sells. It's about audience interaction, encouragement and feedback. You're supposed to be building a community of people with similar interests who share news, ideas and experiences.

A few do's and don'ts:
- Do give more information than you receive.
- Do ask relevant and well-thought-out questions.
- Do catch readers with an attention-getting headline to start your conversation.
- Don't sabotage others' conversations.
- Don't bash your competition.
- Don't update the group about trivial personal matters; rather, start thought-provoking discussions.

Social media and marketing programs
Social media and its use is probably the most important business breakthrough since the industrial revolution. It has

changed the way we buy, try and think about conducting business. It can improve many areas of your business and isn't just limited to marketing. As such, determine the real monetary return on implementing a social media or other marketing campaign. One of the most common performance measurements on any investment is called return on investment, which is used to evaluate one investment over alternative investments.

To calculate ROI, the benefit (return) of an investment is divided by the cost of the investment; the result is expressed as a percentage or a ratio. The formula is:

$$ROI = \frac{(\text{Gain from Investment - Cost of Investment})}{\text{Cost of Investment}}$$

The easiest way to visualize this formula is assume you purchased a $10 stock. Two years later, you sell it for $14.00. The two-year ROI is 40 percent.

In a direct-response marketing campaign, such as the Yellow Pages, direct mail, email or couponing, ROI is easy to calculate. If you're able to identify the revenue that was secured by the campaign (usually by tagging the sales in your accounting system as sourced from that particular campaign), you have the incremental revenue or gain from investment. Because you know what your expenditure was on that particular campaign, evaluating success equates to simply plugging the numbers into the aforementioned formula.

Brand building through billboards, television, radio, public relations, etc., uses the same formula except it's not as easy to identify the gain from the investment because the revenue derived from such a campaign isn't as easily identified most times. Using brand-building marketing techniques, a potential client usually makes his decision after becoming familiar with your company by seeing or hearing this type of advertising multiple times with your name instilled in his mind. When the need for your pest or lawn care service arises, he calls a company he's familiar with.

If your name is in the back of his mind, he might call you. If you ask a customer who has been secured this way how he heard about your company, he can't specifically identify the advertisement that drove him to you. However, the way to measure ROI using brand-building strategies, while perhaps not as specifically identifiable as direct response, can be measured by the increase of revenue during the brand-building campaign versus the total expenditure of the campaign.

Enter social media, which has many qualitative benefits for a company. Everyone in your company is touched by this type of networking several times a day, and many of us forget assembling a social-media strategy is still an investment and needs to be evaluated as such.

Many in the advertising and academia worlds believe the social media discipline is in early development, and as such, traditional financial measurement tools shouldn't be applied to it. However, I disagree.

Unless you can monetize the number of Facebook friends you have, or how large your Linked In group is, or what your Klout score is, we find ourselves ignoring the fact there's a cost-benefit relationship to implementing the program. Many believe that return can be expressed as the number of participants who have friended us or the size of our group. I caution against this type of thinking because this is precisely what drove the Internet bubble of the 1990s. Remember when money didn't matter and it was the number of people who visited a website? Well, many of those companies that relied on eyeballs are gone, and those who understood it was about positive ROI continue to thrive.

So how do you assign value to the intangibility of social media? The aforementioned ROI formula can be used to calculate your return, but the inputs of the formula become much more complex. From a marketing perspective, the return is incremental sales dollars; however, social media provides many additional benefits to a business than incremental sales dollars. While it's clear everything we do in business (i.e., hiring competent staff, using safe treatment techniques, providing customers with accurate information) is done to increase revenue and profit, it can be difficult to quantify how each of these activities add to the top and bottom lines – yet we know they can be drivers of growth.

So, when evaluating our social media strategy, at a minimum, we need to know the expected benefits from implementing such a program. The following is a list of benefits which can be achieved by employing a successful social media strategy:

1. Customer acquisition
2. New sales to existing customers
3. Referrals
4. Decrease of customer problems
5. Website traffic
6. Kew word rankings and related search traffic
7. Employee involvement
8. Reputational issues avoided

Quantifying the aforementioned benefits can be illusive because many on the list are qualitative, but that doesn't mean you shouldn't try – however you need to remember it's your money at risk.

One of most easily quantifiable ROIs financial professionals are able to calculate is in real estate, where we can draw a parallel because residential real estate, for example, has many qualities that can be measured qualitatively and quantitatively. Its ROI is measured easily. The return on residential real estate can be measured by the return you'd receive if you rented the home minus expenses and applying a capitalization rate. Depending on various qualitative factors, including neighborhood, condition, size, etc., you can add to the value of a home, and the value might be assigned at a much higher rate. In this case, the minimum value is the one derived by math. It's the qualitative factors that can potentially add value.

Similarly, with a social media program, you should be able to monetize a potential revenue stream. For every 1,000 Facebook friends, you can sell three new accounts that are worth $600 a year. In this way, we have a measurable return. If the average life of a customer is five years, these three customers will be worth $9,000, not factoring in the time value of money. The question becomes how much was the cost to secure the 1,000 friends. The difference is your return, which can be plugged into the ROI calculation, ignoring all other costs.

In addition to the return you earn from Facebook friends, you might decrease the number of customer problems, your employees might be more engaged in your business and your web traffic might increase. These qualitative items might not be able to be measured easily because they're intangibles, such as the quality of the neighborhood in the real-estate example.

The aforementioned discussion provides a framework that can be used to evaluate an investment in social media and marketing. Above all, a prudent businessperson should, at a minimum, look for the monetary return that can be measured and make a decision based on that. Traditional financial analysis cautions us against making an investment in any endeavor to reap intangible rewards.

Using the ROI model should always give us an acceptable, measurable monetary reward for an investment, be it social media or traditional marketing.

"Efficiency is doing things right; effectiveness is doing the right things."
—*Peter Drucker*

6

EFFECTIVE ROUTING:
How to raise revenues
and decrease expenses

"Hey, Dad. How do we determine who gets serviced and when?" Peter asked. The idea of efficiency was interesting to Peter because he took a course in operations management where he was taught to use decision trees and Gantt charts (which illustrate project schedules) to create the most effective and profitable path to produce a product. In the service business, we don't produce a product; we perform a service-lots of them-each day.

Michael told Peter that when calls come in, Linda schedules them the best she can, and while the routing could probably be more efficient, it's difficult to do when the phone is ringing off the hook, the paperwork never seems to be done and the technicians are needy.

An astute Peter replied that it seems the business will never change if they're constantly doing one-time work that needs to be done yesterday. The beauty of pest control and lawn care businesses is that cycles are predictable, and programs that are performed recurringly can be scheduled far in advance, leaving small gaps in the schedule to accommodate one-time services that can't be avoided. In fact, by plotting stops on a map using software, routing could be optimized to make technicians the most productive, putting the least amount of miles on the trucks and minimizing the amount of fuel used to drive from stop to stop.

Michael knew Peter was right, but didn't know where to start? Michael was learning a lot of theory from his son that seemed to make sense. As a proud father, he couldn't wait for Peter to graduate from business school and join the family business. Michael also knew that much of what Peter was talking about was best handled in computer software. While Michael and Linda knew the basics when it came to operating a computer, they clearly weren't on top of all the new features software companies constantly release. The use of mobile applications and route optimization was becoming more common, and Michael knew he needed to address it to thrive.

Dan's observations and recommendations

Optimize your routing to get the most out of your technicians' time. Efficient routing will keep your technicians on site, providing services to your clients for a higher percentage of the time they're available. This metric of efficiency, called utilization, measures the efficiency of a technician's time. The only thing more important than pricing for profit is efficient routing.

This point will make you or break you!

Even if you were to make $500 per hour, you won't make any money if you only work one hour a day. Your technicians should be as productive as possible, and your managers should stay focused on tightening routes to increase productivity. You can also help increase the effectiveness of your routes by offering your customers a discount for signing up early, which will enable you to schedule more effectively. By booking appointments earlier, you'll know what your routes will look like in advance, which gives you more time to manage and optimize your routes, making the task easier. Aside from keeping your workforce productive, other benefits of efficient routing include gas savings and decreased vehicle wear and tear. Clearly, the benefits of optimized routing are significant.

I'm often asked how a company becomes more profitable. In this world of information overload – of Internet marketing, handheld scanning devices, GPS tracking, hybrid vehicles, cell phone communications and profitability consultants – there are many methods by which a company can become more profitable. Profit increases come down to two factors: increase pricing and lower costs. That's it. All other ideas can work only to increase net profit margin if they can achieve price increases and/or lower costs. So what tool in the service business is more powerful than any other in achieving this objective? Routing. Effective routing will increase revenue and minimize expenses. Let's look at quantitative methods for evaluating route optimization. We know the largest expense in a service business is labor. In the pest control and lawn care industries, there are two methods of compensating technicians: paying hourly (time and a half after 40 hours a week) and paying a percentage of production. There are also hybrid compensation plans that consider hourly and percentage of production.

Fitting more work into less time is at the core of effective route management. This can be done in two ways: by being more efficient when performing the job (taking less time) or reducing windshield time. I don't advocating sacrificing the quality of service by rushing through jobs. I'm advocating better training for treatment techniques, better map use and mapping software, and better management of what we offer customers – our great people.

So, how do you measure efficiency, and how do you benchmark it as a key performance indicator and improve upon it? Let's take a look at a couple of examples.

Example 1
1. A technician earns $15 an hour.
2. Assume he can complete one job (with travel time) in an hour that produces $50
3. In this case, the labor percentage is 30 percent, which means that for every $100 of revenue, there's a $70 profit, ignoring all other costs.
4. It also means we've earned $35 of profit in that hour, ignoring all other costs.

Example 2
1. A technician earns $15 an hour.
2. Assume he can complete two jobs (with travel time) in an hour that produces $50 each or $100 total.
3. In this case, the labor percentage is 15 percent, which means for every $100 of revenue, there's an $85 profit, ignoring all other costs.
4. By fitting more work into less time, we've increased our revenue (from $50 to $100) and decreased our labor cost from 30 to 15 percent.

Remember how to increase profit margins as mentioned in the opening paragraph? Well, using this routing example, we've achieved both – we've increased revenue in total dollars and lowered our cost as a percentage of revenue.

That works where technicians are paid hourly, but what about when technicians are paid as a percent of production? Does it matter how long it takes for a technician to complete his work? Let's look at what can be achieved from better routing using the same logic as examples one and two except in this case a technician is paid as a percentage of production.

Example 3

1. A technician earns 25 percent of production.
2. Assume he can complete one job (with travel time) in an hour that produces $50
3. In this case, profit is $37.50 ($50 – (25% x $50)) (ignoring all other costs).

Example 4

1. A technician earns 25 percent of production.
2. Assume he can complete two jobs (with travel time) in an hour that produces $50 each or $100 total
3. In this case, profit is $75 (($50 x 2) – (25% x $100)) (ignoring all other costs).

By fitting more work into one hour, you're able to increase your profit by $37.50 per hour from $37.50 to $75. In this case, we've increased revenue by $50 per hour while holding our labor expense constant as a percentage of revenue at 25 percent.

In the aforementioned examples, we illustrated that fitting more work into less time makes a business more profitable. While the conclusion is obvious, we used numbers in the calculation and proved it mathematically. But from a managerial standpoint, it becomes difficult to determine if your attempts to improve your routing are working. Without a metric or key performance indicator, quantifying improvements in routing becomes difficult because the dollars per hour on all accounts are rarely the same. By the same token, the dollars per hour received on a particular account isn't an operational issue (unless the workmanship isn't up to snuff), it's a sales issue, meaning the account might not have been sold correctly, resulting in lower dollars per hour. The efficiency with which your customers get serviced is an operational issue. By separating the two issues, a manager can address poor efficiency or pricing in separate conversations.

To determine how efficient we are, we need a method to measure routing efficiency. In accounting, I measure the efficiency of my accountants and bookkeepers using a technique called utilization. Lawyers, accountants and other professionals use this technique as well; however, it fits the pest control and lawn care industry just as well or better.

Here's how it works:

A utilization fraction or percentage is calculated by taking the following quotient:

$$\frac{\text{Total technician hours spent at all stops during the time period}}{\text{Total technician hours clocked in (paid hours) during the time period}}$$

Efficiency example

Let's say your technician spent 30 hours at various jobs working for one week. Let's also assume, according to his time card, he was punched in and paid for 50 hours. His utilization would be 60 percent (30 hours worked / 50 hours clocked in). This means he was producing revenue 60 percent of the time he was clocked in.

Let's assume your average dollar per hour on your accounts for the day is $75. With a 60-percent utilization, you're taking in $45 an hour. If your technician clocks in eight hours for the day, he'll produce $360 for the day ($75 x 60% x 8 hrs).

Assuming his utilization is 75 percent, he'll bring in $450 ($75 x 75% x 8 hrs). If he's 40-percent utilized, he'll bring in $240 ($75 x 40% x 8 hrs). These numbers use the same $75 per hour but varying the utilization percentage.

There are only two ways to increase profit margins: price increases or cost savings. Any tools that can be employed to achieve either one might be a sound investment. Efficient routing is the most powerful tool in a PCO or lawn care business to achieve this. There are many pieces of software on the market that can help with this. The method to judge the effectiveness of your efforts is by calculating utilization.

Another way to help increase the effectiveness of your routes is by offering customers a discount for signing up early, which will enable you to schedule more effectively. By booking appointments earlier you will know in advance what your routes will look like. This gives you more time to manage and optimize your routes, making the task easier.

Design your programs so there are more choices for you when developing routes. For example, rather than scheduling a home service at a specific time, why not offer the service as a convenience to the customer, providing outside and inside services when requested. This way, you allow the appointment to be scheduled when it best fits into your schedule and you're not locked into a specific time to perform service.

Remember, to promote efficiency, measure results continuously because this is the only way you can tell if your business decisions are effective. Identify the metrics that will provide you with the insight needed to help make important business decisions. Once you determine what to measure and how to go about doing it, don't stop.

When it comes to marketing, measuring results is important. This concept needs to be applied to the operational areas of your business as well. Identify what needs to be measured in your company. This might include categories such as sales, labor rates, direct cost versus fixed cost, marketing cost, net profit, etc. These categories can be seen as your business' key performance indicators (KPI), which show you how you're doing at any given point and provide insight into the health of your organization.

Have the data presented to you monthly. The data presented will be determined by what type of business lines you offer. Identify your KPIs, and understand why they're considered KPIs for your business. Keep measuring, and don't stop.

"Never call an accountant a credit to his profession; a good accountant is a debit to his profession."

—*Charles Lyell*

ACCOUNTING AND FINANCE:
Business is a game;
do you know the score?

Michael wanted nothing to do with the accounting aspect of the business. Linda was able to do the daily bookkeeping using a system she developed throughout the years, but the problem was only she knew how to decipher what was recorded. Michael looked at accounting as a necessary evil, but get him on the golf course and he could spend plenty of time with his CPA.

The Halls visited the accountant a couple times a year. The

first visit, the accountant would request the proper documents to put financial statements together, usually lecturing Michael and Linda about how, if they did this earlier in the year, the last-minute fire drill could be avoided. One of the things Peter understood well from his success at business school was organization is everything. Setting up a filing system – be it in the file cabinet or a virtual file system – is the only way to verify any work, plans, financial transactions or other items that need to be recalled at a later date.

While the Halls relied on their CPA to prepare their taxes and financial statements, their CPA relied on the Halls to provide the documentation to compile and confirm the information needed to create those statements. The torture Linda put herself through each year at tax time was clearly caused by her lack of understanding of how to set up an effective filing system for permanent documents, as well as documents that relate to the fiscal year and documents needed to prove the financial information each month. Peter decided it was time to help his mom.

"Mom, these records are a mess," he said. "This weekend, I'm going to help you organize them and get the information needed to make sure the records are orderly and complete."

Peter had taken financial accounting and had a solid understanding that monthly accounting and bookkeeping was like showering. It needed to be done at least every day. Peter explained to Linda accounting could be looked at on several levels. From top down, financial statements where the culmination of the process that was produced through a daily recording of transactions, including customer invoices, payments, vendor checks, payroll, recording of credit card expenses and monthly bank reconciliations.

Linda understood all this and had her own way of performing these tasks but did them on her own time. The problem was her time rarely coincided with a regular schedule, which created tension between her and Michael. When he had the time, he was interested in how his business was performing and looked for Linda to give him financial reports. But to maintain peace, he rarely pushed Linda because he knew she was busy.

Dan's observations and recommendations

Accounting is the language that communicates the health of a business. When many people think of accounting, they think of April 15, tax day. However, there's much more to the accounting function, regarding the company owner, than taxes. A competent CPA should be able to file taxes and prepare statements for banks, creditors and other stakeholders in a business. He also should be able to help create budgets and represent you in a tax audit.

The overall goal of your accountant should be to help you accumulate and preserve wealth. Saving taxes is just a small part of the task. A competent accountant recognizes he needs to be a valuable member of his client's management team and is able to provide many more value-added services than just tax preparation. A growing company needs help with many of the financial aspects of its business.

As your business grows, you need the internal structure and financial controls to support the growth. This aspect of accounting is called management accounting, which has to do with compiling and reporting information needed to improve the results of an operation.

Many CPAs are in a unique position to help business owners in this area by helping them to set up procedures to accurately record the daily transactions associated with doing business and by observing the company and comparing that information to other clients with whom they work. An accountant should be a trusted member of the management team, providing the owner information to improve the efficiency of the business. The following are essential elements of the inside accounting function required to run a successful service business.

Preparing financial statements

Financial statements are the culmination of the accounting process. They're used to convey a concise picture of the profitability and financial position of the company. The two most important financial statements that allow you to get an accurate snap shot of the results of your business are the:

- profit and loss statement (P&L); and the
- balance sheet.

The P/L shows how much profit or loss a company generated for a given period. But more importantly, it shows how that profit or loss was derived by category of expense and revenue. It's extremely important an accountant understand the service business because certain financial benchmarks are used to rate businesses using this terminology that are unique to the pest control and green industries.

A growing service company that uses a generic chart of accounts is at a distinct disadvantage to larger companies who use their chart of accounts to generate financial statements, which allow them to analyze their businesses and answer important questions such as:

- Is my material expense in line with my revenue?
- Is my direct labor cost in line with my overall revenues?
- Am I spending more or less as a percentage of revenues than the average company on advertising?
- What percentage of my revenue do I spend on running my office?
- What are my vehicle costs as a percentage of revenues?
- I know I spend a lot on overtime, but do I spend too much on overtime?

The balance sheet shows the financial position of a company on a given date (i.e., assets, liabilities and net worth). An easy way to distinguish the P/L from the balance sheet is to think of the P/L as a statement showing how the business performed in terms of revenue, profit and growth for a given period. The balance sheet shows what the company is worth as a result of all cumulative P/Ls and financing activities in the past as a banker would look at it. Remember, your customer list isn't included on your balance sheet in most cases. Usually this has more value than anything else in your business. Most bankers don't look at this as an asset when making lending decisions.

Setting Up Financial Statements

The entire accounting system is organized around a chart of accounts. Think of a chart of accounts as all the different categories of deposits or expenses you write in the memo section of your checkbook. All entries in your checkbook then are added up by these categories and the profit-and-loss and balance sheet are created, incorporating all these transactions. In this manner, a standard chart of accounts allows you to categorize all inflows and out flows of money entering and exiting your business.

Therefore, it's important you set up your chart of accounts to match your financial reporting objectives. The first step is creating your chart of accounts so it enables the proper visibility and accuracy when determining whether or not your business is on the right track. It sounds simple, but the more information you want in your reporting the more complex your chart of accounts becomes. You should exercise some restraint when designing your chart of accounts because to much detail clouds the big picture.

So, how do you set up a chart of accounts for a service business? Here's the basic structure of a typical chart of accounts:

Income. How do you measure your income? What you're interested in is your recurring revenue. This is where the value of your business is derived. You can break your revenue up by division – commercial vs. residential for example, which will give you insight into your client mix.

Variable/direct costs. What are your direct or variable costs? This is the cost of putting a technician on the road. Direct costs vary with the volume of work you do. The more work you do, the higher the variable costs. Some examples of variable costs include technician payroll costs, worker's comp, uniforms, truck leases, fuel, materials, etc.

Marketing costs. Marketing and sales costs usually are grouped together. However, these items are separate and distinct. Marketing is defined as all activity that helps bring a lead into your company. Sales is all activity created to close that lead. Marketing and sales costs, while belonging under the same major heading, need to be tracked separately.

General and administrative costs. This includes items such as rent, utilities, office supplies, etc. The general and administrative costs are usually your fixed costs, which can be defined as those costs incurred regardless of how much or little work you sell.

The internal accounting function is extremely important. Having precise, reliable and insightful information is critical to your business' success. Your internal accountant/bookkeeper is the gatekeeper to this information, so make sure you have a solid internal person and then include him or her in your management team's decision-making process.

Having a Strong Accountant/Bookkeeper

A strong internal accountant / bookkeeper can help spot trends in your business such as material, labor or marketing cost spikes. Your internal accountant / bookkeeper should understand these expense items proper relationships to revenue and determine how they should be presented in your financial statements. Now, we know materials may be a big expense in your service business; but by watching the materials, you can tell a lot about your company. For example, are your people stealing materials from the business? Are your technicians over-applying or under-applying materials?

Marketing is another area where accurate financial information can make a huge difference. A skillful accountant/ bookkeeper can tell you which one of the three advertising campaigns you've implemented didn't work. Now you can eliminate the ineffective campaign and reduce your advertising cost. These are just some of the examples of what a strong internal accountant / bookkeeper can do for you and why it's important to have a strong person performing the internal accounting function. You'll need someone with a solid strategic financial background. So how do you know if you have the right accountant? Trial and error, but most of all, look for results.

Your Accounting Software

You should use your accounting software to increase visibility in your business. Your information is only as good as the functionality of your accounting systems. By using the current technology that's widely available, it's easy for you to gain visibility into your business' performance. But beware of the pitfalls of chinsing on accounting software purchases. This is an area where your money is well spent because the information derived from your accounting system is invaluable.

Technology is improving every day. Many of the functions you can do in a computer system used to be done by hand. Bank statements used to be typed on typewriters and reconciled by hand. Now, the technology is so sophisticated and affordable, everyone can afford an accurate and efficient accounting system. For example, QuickBooks is a versatile accounting program that allows users to increase visibility into their businesses. With the right data and tools, the sky's the limit.

The bottom line is to be diligent when entering your company's data. I can't stress this enough. Make sure you fill in all the necessary cells and understand what computers can do.

Talk to your accountant to determine what information is important and which fields need to be populated. The more data you collect and the more accurate it is, the better off you'll be. You'll soon be enabled to slice your data in a number of different ways, helping you make well-informed business decisions with the greatest of ease.

When you want to know what happened in a baseball game, what do you do? You read the box score in the newspaper. It summarizes the activity and results for the game. Your financial statements serve the same purpose. It lets you know how your business is performing. Make sure you review them so you can make educated guesses, which will help guide you in making key business decisions. Make sure your company is set up right so you can track things like who has the most production, who's selling the most and who's closing at the highest rate. When you have all this information, it's like you're reading the box scores of a baseball game. And from these numbers, you can make educated and informed decisions. The numbers are facts, and they don't lie. So if you're going to trust the numbers, make sure you have an accurate, reliable accounting system you can depend on.

Protecting your company from Tax audits

Protect yourself from audits by keeping accurate records. Receipts, invoices, work orders, bank statements, credit card statements, check stubs, and ledgers … make sure you hang on to these and file them away where they're easily accessible. Much of this information will be passed back and forth between you and your accountant, so make sure you know where it is. These items are proof of your company's transactions, and you might be asked to reproduce them in the case you're audited. Keep excellent records, because if you don't, you'll get hit with penalties, interest and back taxes when the auditors come in.

Here's the way an audit works. When an auditor comes into the office, he'll select a period of time and check every transaction during that period. If you're organized and he's confident everything is in order, you'll come out with flying colors.

The biggest problem with a growing company is owners sometimes don't organize their information properly. Then, when the auditor sees the company is in disarray, he'll say, "This is missing, so you owe taxes on it" and "That's missing, so you owe taxes on it." If he thinks the records are inaccurate and disorganized, he'll open up the audit period and look at a larger sample period; and he'll check it more in depth during the expanded sample period. This could be like opening a big can of worms.

Recordkeeping is important because you want to avoid confusing an auditor. Make sure everything is in line when the auditor arrives.

Planning

Stay in tune with your numbers. Check your financial outlook no matter what your company's size. You must know where the business stands financially at all times. Monitor your financials at least once a day to help maintain your business like a machine. It's like having a car; you need to change the oil and tune it up. Make improvements to your business, not just for growth, but also for survival. As you monitor your business' vital metrics, give your company tune-ups by adjusting your business with growth in mind.

By staying tuned in to your financial picture, you comprehend the interaction between the various areas of your finances to the point where you know what needs to be measured. Create measurements for each item important to you and the success of your business. If you're unsure about what needs to be measured, consult your accountant to understand the vital metrics in your financial statements.

Budget your way to success by understanding your revenue and expenses

Pest and lawn care revenue can be categorized into three main areas: route work, new sales and renewals. When setting up your budget, it's important to enable your organization to monitor these revenue groups individually.

We sell recurring revenue service contracts, and by making a few calculations, we can predict, with great accuracy, how much revenue we're going to produce for the year. New sales are the wildcard, but we can even predict them with some accuracy as well based on historic factors. That's the top line, which will dictate your cost structure and how much you'll spend on labor, trucks and other direct costs. We also can estimate these costs with pinpoint accuracy. Therefore, when we carefully craft our budget, we can usually forecast future profit and loss with a high degree of accuracy. When you create a budget every year, you'll know information such as how many technicians you need, the cost of each technician, and how much advertising to do.

There's hardly any other business that exists in which you can be so accurate because of the predictability of a recurring revenue model, which makes budgeting in the PCO and lawn care industry an accurate exercise and an ideal tool for business planning. Not creating a budget is like driving down a dark street at night with your headlights off. There's no way to see what's coming down the street and no way to tell if you'll drive into something.

When developing your budget, make it reasonable regarding revenues and expenses, know what you're planning to spend money on, prioritize your major expenditures, and revisit your budget periodically. While going through this exercise, make a list of areas you can improve.

Everything falls into place when you start tracking and measuring your numbers. You might find yourself in a situation where you need to show banks a certain amount of profit at the end of the year. You need to have this budgeting framework mapped out because it helps you plan and work toward your objectives for the coming year.

Once you make the sales forecast, budget all the expenses. If you don't create a budget, you could find yourself taking on a lot debt because you won't have the sales to support your expenses. You need to understand what your sales are going to be to understand what your expenses will be. Budgeting can help you get through each season because it gives you something to compare. Budgeting can help you make pricing decisions regardless of your size.

Finally, when you create a budget, it needs to be realistic. It can't be too aggressive because that can hurt morale, but it can help develop better managers. Give your top-level managers a piece of the budget to be responsible for. Let the managers take care of the details and watch them grow into profit-minded leaders in your organization.

Create a procedure for keeping your expenses in check such as employee expense reports. This will help monitor how much money your business is spending as well as hold employees accountable for what they spend. Identify reasons for large increases and decreases in spending and note whether they're justified.

Many small-business owners think they can outsell their expenses. Yet there are some expenses that have a tendency to spiral out of control. As your business grows, many of these expenses tend to grow as well. It's important you monitor and control these costs no matter how good sales appear to be.

Keep your expenses in check by collecting expense reports from all employees that incur expenses. Make sure these expense items are entered into your accounting system and monitored regularly. Also, monitor activity on corporate cards used by employees. When credit card statements come in, look at each transaction and make note of unfamiliar vendors or expenses that look out of the ordinary.

Try reducing costs by reducing fixed overhead. Many

companies perform a break-even analysis and since fixed overhead is a significant part of the equation, any reduction in overhead reduces your breakeven point. By reducing your breakeven point you reduce the number of service contracts you need to sell to reach profitability, which means your business will start generating income a lot sooner when overhead is minimized.

Understand the moment when you get over the break-even point is when you start generating a lot of income. So if you could get to the break-even point sooner, you'll be making money a lot sooner.

Look at the present versus the past, and compare your expenses for the current period versus an earlier period and note any differences. It's useful to do this for year-to-year and month-to-month comparisons. This will quickly point out whether your business is improving or getting worse.

First off, if you're not familiar with the terms, here's basic accounting lingo for accounting periods. For this example, let's assume today's date is June 15, 2013.

- **Year-to-date**
  Includes all business activity from Jan. 1, 2013 to June 15, 2013
- **Month-to-date**
  Includes all business activity from June 1, 2013 to June 15, 2013
- **Fiscal year**
  The 12-month period a business uses to define a full year of activity for accounting purposes
- **Calendar year**
  The one-year period beginning Jan. 1 and ending Dec. 31

You can tell a lot by looking at where you are on a year-to-date basis and comparing that number to where you were last year at the same date. Another worthwhile comparison is where you are on a month-to-date basis compared to the same month-to-date period the previous year. Comparing the current year to previous years provides you a big-picture understanding of long-term trends and helps you create future plans. Both of these comparisons are insightful when looking at whole years and months as well. But be careful not to confuse the month-to-month comparison as this month to last month (e.g. June 2013 to May 2013). Because the service business is seasonal, this comparison won't tell you much. The comparison we're referring to is June 2013 to June 2012.

Compare your financial results against industry standards. It's always nice to know how you're doing compared to your competition. For example, knowing how much the average service provider spends on labor will allow you to see how you stack up against others in the industry. Doing such comparisons throughout your profit-and-loss statement will help you recognize areas of your business that might be mismanaged. On the flip side, you also might spot areas where you're not spending enough and can afford to do so.

Getting a hold of industry financial standards isn't easy in the service industry because so many businesses are privately owned. Unfortunately for small businesses there's no overseeing organization like the SEC to standardize and monitor financial statements. Unfortunately, this means there's not much financial data about other companies to reference for your purposes, but that's not to say the information can't be gathered.

Look in your neighbor's yard

One of the benefits of using a service success coaching program is all members use the same chart of accounts, which ensures they're all on a level playing field. They compare apples to apples, which makes comparisons meaningful and valuable. Our firm offers coaching services, please contact us for more information.

Now you can see how you compare to the crowd, which will enable you to see which areas your business excels and which areas you need to improve. Going through this exercise is a valuable and eye-opening experience. It's like opening your own Pandora's Box – you might not like what you see, but once you see your company's blemishes, you'll be forced to make a change. How could you live with yourself otherwise?

Tally your service-contract count

Because your service contracts are the focal point of your business' value, it's important to know how many service contracts you have. This will give you a general idea of the size of your portfolio of clients.

Has anyone ever asked you how big your business is? What's your answer? Is that an up-do-date answer, or is it based on last year's numbers? Here's an example of the back-of-the-envelope approach: I know I have 10,000 clients on service programs that average about $500 per year. So, in two seconds, I can tell you my business generates about $5 million in revenue.

What this approach also tells me is those 10,000 clients are repeat clients. We get renewals every year and can count on that business. Therefore, this $5-million revenue number indicates a certain level of wealth stored in the business.

Remember, those service contracts are the heart of your company. That's next year's revenue. That's next year's work queue. It's fantastic to constantly know where you stand in service contracts. This is one of the most critical stats for you to monitor in your business because these contracts are the foundation of your company and its worth.

Watch for the number of contracts you have now, how you're growing the number of contracts, and what time of the year these contracts are sold. This is a great tool to know how you're doing financially and how to staff your workforce, manage seasonality, and develop growth potential for your service business.

Customer retention: It's a game of percentages

Know what your customer retention rate is because it will

tell you how well your clients like your company and value your company's services. This also will help you forecast your company's top line in the future, making budgeting exercises more accurate and reliable.

What if you could retain 100 percent of your customer base? It will never happen. Customers leave for many reasons, and it's not always because of customer service. Think of your customer base as a herd. You're the shepherd, and it's your job to keep the herd together. Every once in a while, one of your sheep is going to stray. It's just a fact. So, when customers cancel their contract, you need to know why. Put together a list of cancellations. Calculate your retention percentage as the number of clients you have this year that stayed with your service divided by the number of clients you had last year. Don't count this year's new clients in this calculation.

If your cancellation percentage seems high, know what to do about it. Have a system in place whereby you collect customer information. If you can have a customer service representative perform a brief customer feedback survey, you'll be able to collect valuable information about your cancellations. If you have a high number of cancellations, take action. Listen to your clients and determine if there's a flaw in your services. Or, maybe you're lacking something your competition has. This can be a telling stat. But no matter what the results are, don't take bad news personally and rest on your laurels in light of good news. Know high retention is a product of your company's consistent delivery of quality and value to your customers. Know your true cost of labor. There might be hidden costs you don't factor into your labor cost. For example, there are costs associated with recruiting, training, benefits, vacation, sick time, insurance, and so on. It's important to know how much these expenses truly are.

When you hire labor, and it doesn't work out, you have invested a lot of money. If you're paying for employee benefits such as sick time, personal days, vacations and holidays, understand your pay rate is higher than your hourly wage.

It's important to know your labor costs, so think about the benefits you give your employees, not to mention payroll taxes, training, insurance, uniforms and intangibles, such as your time.

Labor is the biggest expense in your business, so manage it properly. Keeping your labor costs under control is difficult. Your company's total labor accounts for more than 45 percent of your costs, which easily is the largest cost you have on your profit-and-loss statement.

Assemble the best team you can find, and make your labor force as productive as possible. Give each employee the right amount of work so they can produce more revenue, enabling you to pay them the right amount. Make each employee a profitable entity within your business, and make sure you can financially justify each member of your organization because the cost to carry each employee is too high to bear unless that employee is productive.

Know how much your customers cost. It takes money to make money. There are definitely costs associated with bringing in new customers, and those costs include advertising, sales efforts, promotional programs, and the labor involved in initial client set up. These costs can add up, so know what the total is, and factor this into your pricing. Furthermore, just as with gaining new customers, it takes money to service existing customers. Understanding the cost components included in delivering your service can be a major eye-opener for you and how you choose to operate and sell your services.

Determine what the marketing cost is to bring in a new customer. You're probably going to lose money during the first year; but in year two, these clients become very profitable if priced correctly. This is your incentive to boost your customer retention.

So, what does it cost to carry this customer and provide outstanding service? You have to figure this out; otherwise, how do you know if you're price is even high enough to make a profit?

The best way to determine this is by determining what it costs to perform service on an hourly basis. Then, determine how long it takes to perform each customer's service. Ask yourself these questions, and explore how profitable each client is as an individual account.

- How many hours did you spend performing services for this client?
- How many times did you have to visit the client's home or business?
- Is this client keeping your employees on the phone constantly and making them unproductive?
- Look at the averages and ask yourself if you're spending more or less time with this client than the average?
- Is this client an outlier in any cost category?

Asking these types of questions will help you spot clients sucking up your resources. You might even find you're losing money with some of these clients.

To correct this, address the problems that cause them to be resource hogs. If you can't adjust to bring the client back in line, raise their price until they're profitable for you to service or they go away. One of the most uncomfortable things for an entrepreneur to do is to fire customers, yet sometimes that's exactly what needs to be done.

"We're in a simple business – not an easy business but a simple business."
—*Dan Gordon, CPA*

OPERATIONS AND SYSTEMATIZING YOUR BUSINESS

As a business student, high school football player and admirer of winning teams, Peter developed a philosophy that greatness can't be achieved without a plan. When discussing this with his dad, he communicated the plan needs to be codified in a playbook. Football teams use playbooks to create winning offenses, defenses and special teams. Business plans contain road maps to expanding businesses. At the operational level, where business is done and services are performed, there must be a policy and procedure manual. In essence, a playbook that illustrates how to complete jobs by all employees in all functional areas, such as office and sales procedures, technical and nontechnical training, and monthly bookkeeping. The playbook explains what needs to be done and who will perform the functions.

When Peter asked Michael what, if any, documentation existed, Michael, somewhat embarrassed, explained the business school stuff is helpful, but work needs to be done in a limited amount of time. Peter understood that if he was to take over the business someday, all these concepts needed to be implemented. So he committed to his father that he, during the next few years, would work on transitioning the company from a small entrepreneurial business where most decisions were made based on how the owner felt that day to a professionally run organization that implements concepts taught at business schools. After all, he wanted to make his mark on the business and the community. Peter was committed.

Dan's observations and recommendations
Systematize your business

Your company does a number of things well. They can be as general as marketing or as specific as routing. Whatever these activities are, they need to be systematized so the business continues to perform them well in the future. This will help strengthen these tasks and develop a foundation for the company on which to build.

Pick something you're good at, and systematize it. In fact, you should make sure you have a system for everything you're trying to do. But for now, let's stick to one process – the one you're best at. Write it down and codify it so anybody can perform and repeat the process.

The most difficult thing to do is write down each step. Make sure you're as specific as possible. It has to be dummy proof so you and your employees can deliver a consistent, repetitive service that drives the economic engine you're operating – your service business.

You want the process to be in a format you can print and put in a book or a binder. Build a manual you can hand to new employees as you expand. This will help train them about the acceptable policies and procedures that your company follows.

In this manner, each service, as well as each step to process new sales, accounting and other paper work, can be performed in a uniform manner. Using this approach, you can build your business machine in a way that's entirely systematized. Once you've reached this point, where the business is completely systematized and the work is performed entirely by your workforce, you can start working on growth strategies for the future as well as how those strategies will be implemented.

Start with the low-hanging fruit, and systematize your services. It's something you do well. You have mastered it, so now you have to put it on paper and make all your employees master it, too.

When doing this exercise, know what it's going to look like when it's done. Build it like a machine. Beginning with an end in mind will give you an idea of what you're trying to accomplish. Now you have to create a procedure to make it all happen.

Now that you've systematized what you are good at, improve and systematize those activities that you're not good at. At this point, you're plugging the holes in the boat and, hopefully, turning weaknesses into strengths.

Look at your business in functional areas. You have operations, marketing and sales, accounting and finance, and employee management. Be sure there are no gaps in your systems and every procedure in your business is captured.

You're not perfect. Now, of course, you can't be good at everything. You might need to invest in the talent you need to fill in the gaps in your organization and eliminate some of the weaknesses.

Improve your capabilities. Or sometimes you can turn these weaknesses into strengths or competencies. Many times you'll find that merely systematizing a process can be helpful to turn weaknesses into strengths. This is where a lot of learning comes into play. Exploring a process that you're not extremely familiar with can help you understand it better. The more you try new things and the more repetitions you go through, the more comfortable you'll be with the process.

Borrow from others. Look at other people's systems and procedures. They might not be exactly what you're looking for, but it's likely a sound starting point from which you can build. You might even be able to take the process and add your own twist, applying it differently.

A well-planned office setup helps a successful organization. The way you set up your office is vital to helping your organization. Everything from filing systems to intercom configurations can make your company's workforce efficient and productive. Think through every minute detail, from the flow of traffic through the office to the positioning of phone and data jacks.

Organize your workflow

Organizing your office and workflow is paramount to executing a sustainable growth model. Think about the workflow of your business and how that impacts your office. Remember, there are two areas of consideration in office setup – the physical setup (office space, desks, chairs, water coolers, phones, faxes and computers) and the dynamic flow of information (incoming calls, voicemails, emails, instant messaging, intercoms, escalating and filing paperwork).

Setting up the physical office

Where do you start? Ask yourself questions about how your business operates:

- When phone calls are received, whom do they go to and how are they answered?

- How are technicians or salespeople who go to customers' houses informed?
- How is work posted?
- What paperwork comes back to the office after services are performed?
- How do you file paperwork?
- How do you bill customers?
- How do you process payments?

This is merely a small sampling of activities that needs to be worked out. Think through your company's specific workflow and plan your office accordingly.

Handling incoming requests and inquiries

Organizing phone calls is a big task. The way you organize the flow of phone calls can be difficult, but it's important. Set up an automated call system so the number of calls that goes to the front desk is minimal. Every call will be routed to the appropriate customer service representative (CSR).

Have CSRs become experts on all your service programs so each one knows every particular aspect of the service that your company offers. You want your CSRs to be knowledgeable and develop relationships with clients because when clients call, they speak to a CSR who knows and understands them as well as the best solution recommended to solve their problem.

Another way to manage incoming traffic is to use an instant messaging service on your website for those who don't want to wait on the phone. Customers can get a hold of a rep online with the click of the mouse.

Chat time and the design of your office

We know employee chat time is a common problem for business owners. At the end of the day, technicians often return to the office after a long day and want to chat with the CSRs. Granted, technicians are done for the day, but chat time can be unproductive for the CSRs and become a hindrance to the business. So, design your workspace so the technicians have a separate area where they can congregate without interrupting the CSRs during their busiest times - at the beginning and end of the day. This will help ensure the phone gets answered when it rings and the office remains efficient and productive.

When setting up your office, the little things can make employee and customer experiences more rewarding and help grow your business by adding value.

The right person for inbound sales calls

Find the right person to answer the phone. That person needs to be engaging and able to close a deal. Just doing a little bit better can help a lot. For example, let's say the person answering the phones sells a couple more service contracts each day. This will result in hundreds of more clients by the end of the season.

Answering the phones is the first encounter or engagement people will have with your company. This is your front line. Having the right people in the right area is critical.

CSRs vs salespeople

Make sure you distinguish between your CSRs and salespeople. CSRs must be good listeners and should be independent, strong-willed people who can deal with an upset, scared or frustrated customer. They must be able to resolve problems efficiently.

Understand the role of a CSR is different from the role of a salesperson, who should be relegated to sales activity. A good salesperson should be able to sell a customer on your premier programs all day long. They need to use an assortment of sales techniques to make the sale and overcome customer objections. Salespeople must get complete information from the customer to make sure the contact information and other data in your computer system is complete. They must know how to talk about services and work those discussions into a final sale.

Training is definitely involved but having the right mindset is also important.

On-the-road vs. over-the-phone sales

Many companies don't sell over the phone. They send reps out into the field. But the bottom line is it's difficult to find a good salesperson who can and will close sales and not just take orders. You can try having technicians sell, but many times that isn't as effective as having a dedicated sales-person. What we've found is there's a conflict in the job duties. Technicians who sell the work eventually have to do the work. If it's a job they don't want, they won't push for the sale. So create division in your job responsibilities. The people selling the new business shouldn't be the ones who have to do the work.

There's debate in the industry about which sales approach works best - on the road sales-people or in office telesales-people. You could put a dedicated salesperson on the road, but this approach has many downsides as well. Many times, salespeople will end up selling services to the lowest common denominator at a minimum price. They might not sell add-on services. Still, the commissions you have to pay them can be high.

We've found a better approach is to hire telephone salespeople, and track over-the-phone salespeople the same way you track on-the-road salespeople using daily sales and lead reports. This is important because it can increase the volume of sales you can drive per day. For example, how many stops can a road sales-person cover in a day? Perhaps eight to 10 at most. How many phone calls can a phone sales-person make or answer in a day? It could be five or six an hour. If you do this correctly, your telesales person can generate millions of dollars over the phone without even leaving his desk.

Create a playbook of sales techniques for consistent and repeatable results. Sales scripts, which can be used for many different types of selling, work great with a telesales-person because it creates an easy reference when they're on the phone and helps when a customer asks about a service, payment terms or other items that will help make a sale. Additionally, if you identify a list of negative objections that clients or potential clients bring up you have a canned answer to their objection. No matter what your sales script's application might be, it always pays to be prepared.

The perfect salesperson

Picture your perfect employee. How does he speak? What if you could capture that perfection in a bottle and clone that employee? You probably would if you could. So, assuming we're past the idea of cloning employees, the next best thing is writing scripts so your entire workforce speaks the same way. We've talked about systematizing your company and its processes, and here's another area where this can be done. Here's a short list of scripts and protocols that can add value to your business' front line:

1. Answer the phone
2. Lead a phone call
3. How to sell a program
4. How to sell an add-on service
5. How to upsell services
6. How to cross-sell services
7. Telemarketing scripts
8. Inbound sales call scripts
9. Possible rebuttals to sales objections
10. Playbook of words and phrases to use and not use

As an aside, when writing scripts, make them as brief as possible without compromising their effectiveness. Don't have open-ended questions that give room for unnecessary gab in conversation because it will only take that much longer for the sales rep to move onto the next sales opportunity. Even 20 extra seconds in a script multiplied by 50 calls a day and a team of reps ... you can see how a minor adjustment in a script can have an exponential impact on the effectiveness and productivity of your inbound sales force.

Service contracts

The name of the game is selling service contracts. To build your business this way, you have to convert your current clients to service programs as well as sell all new clients service contracts. Communicate the value of your program, sell the benefits, and then sign them up. The conversion process isn't always smooth, but it's worth it.

Sell an annual commitment and don't waiver on your renewals. Call your customers continuously to get those annual renewals. You can offer special promotions and gifts. Call them, send them mailings, email your customers, do whatever it takes to engage the customer. Remember, servicing clients is a relationship business. Make sure you maintain that relationship.

You need to have your customers buying into the fact they need to be on a regular maintenance program. People want peace of mind knowing everything is going to be protected. You can offer that to them. But people can't get peace of mind by purchasing a one-time service. That's not how it works. That peace of mind is included in your service programs.

Unfortunately, as you will find, people are naturally resistant to change. If you've built your business on one-time jobs, it might be possible that many of your clients are using your services because the other service providers in your area only offer service programs. So, perhaps they are your customers only because you offer one-time jobs. When you call those people, they initially might think they don't need a regular service.

Don't let your customers dictate how you're going to work. You have to re-educate these clients. Communicate the benefits of a regular maintenance plan. Talk about how some treatments degrade in sunlight or why periodic inspections around a client's home are required. While going through this process, you'll find yourself in an uphill battle, and you'll lose customers. But your average revenue per customer will increase, your book of clients will be more stable, your customer retention will improve year to year, and best of all, you'll set up your business to store more value in the long run.

When you go to the grocery store, there are products in the aisles, promotional items on the end caps, and inventory at the checkout lines. Your business should take this model and incorporate it into your sales process.

Customers have to be reminded and asked if they'd like to add services to their order. To be good at upselling your customers, develop a process that enables you to seize every opportunity that comes your way. This process must be codified and become second nature to your entire staff, from managers, to sales people, to CSRs, to technicians.

The by-the-way sale

Let's say you inspect for pests and notice the homeowner has a deck. Perhaps you offer a power washing, deck sealing or lawn care service. Remember to sell what you were called there to sell but try to sell the added services as well either now or in the future.

Many sales people blow leads because they throw a handful of proposals at a customer. A decision on a $500 job becomes a decision about a multiservice job with a $3,000 price tag. This is confusing and overwhelming for the customer and is a sure-bet way to ruin the sale. Nurture the customer you may get the full $3000 sale but it may come in steps.

A salesperson needs to be organized and take customers down a particular path. If you're on a call for one problem, design a solution, promote your product and get the deal endorsed. Then, depending on how smoothly the initial sale went, and if you have developed a good connection with the customer, use your by-the-way sales pitch.

"By the way, when inspecting, I noticed you have a deck out back. We offer power washing and deck sealing. We can power wash it and seal it with UV light protection. We offer a three-year warranty on the railings and a two-year warranty on the flats. Would you like to discuss that further?" Don't be pushy, but just put it out there to see if there's interest.

Here are a few more by-the-way pitches:

- "By the way, we're running a special this month on grub control ..."
- "By the way, we're coming out to do the lawn next week, and we'd love to be able to do a treatment for the mosquito or tick activity in the area ..."
- "By the way, for a limited time, we're offering a free $50 gift card for clients who sign up for our premier service program ..."

Devise your own pitches based on the programs and specials you offer, but remember, the story has to make sense, and there has to be a plot.

Setting up technology and information management

Technology and computer hardware can be your best friend and your worst enemy. Cell phones, tablets, GPS devices, laptops, you name it, there are all sorts of technology tools available that can increase productivity and enable your business. On the other hand, poor planning, lack of knowledge, or improperly applying products technology can be a hindrance. The key is finding the right places to implement technology solutions and how to do it.

If you can increase productivity with technology, it's worth it. There are many great nice-to-have technologies, but the key is to make sure costs are under control and you don't spend too much time implementing the technology. You can't have technology run your business. If you don't have willpower and discipline, you might find yourself implementing technology just for the sake of it, which isn't what you want to do.

Technological solutions must be deployed to serve a business need. The only reason to use technology should be to improve your business. If the technology doesn't move you closer to your business goal, perhaps you should hold off on the initiative.

Manage your information meticulously, and it will become one of your company's greatest assets. If there's any time you want to let your obsessive-compulsive disorder take over, it's when you deal with your company's information. Be meticulous when collecting and organizing information about your employees, trucks, equipment, finances, expenses, and any other information you deem useful. Having information you can rely on will help you make educated business decisions confidently.

You have to be detail oriented. There's no way around it. There are so many business owners who are constantly running around putting out fires they don't have the time to manage their data correctly. They need to pause for a minute to make sure they collect robust, accurate information at the moment when the opportunity arises.

Collect data about your people and equipment. Data collection is about creating a detailed information system that helps you understand maintenance needs or how much production a technician is capable of producing.

Think about how you want to organize your information. If you omit getting it, it's difficult to return and get it later. Start this habit when your business is small because it becomes a monumental task once your business grows.

Garbage in, garbage out

When you take on this data collection task, let your OCD kick into overdrive and be meticulous to the point where you annoy everyone around you. You want to know the mileage on all your trucks, when your technicians' driver's licenses expire, every detail about the inventory you have - you want to know it all!

Your data has to be comprehensive and reliable. If you

have a bad database with misspelled words and inaccurate or incomplete information, you won't be able to trust it when you want to use the information as a basis for making an important business decision.

Develop checklists to cover all bases. Checklists are a business' best friend. This is how you ensure oversights and eliminate errors. Systems need the proper controls in place to make them airtight and dependable.

It's insufficient to have a checkmark next to a task. Have a checkmark and spot where someone initials a task so you know who did it. Record the date when the task was completed and then make note of any follow-up that's necessary. Here's an example of items listed on a checklist used to close each month:

- Generate a sales report that shows revenue by service.
- Print a payment report with all deposits.
- Print a sales tax report to show in which jurisdictions you've collected sales tax and to whom you have to remit.
- Put all that information into the general ledger system.
- Look through each account step by step to make sure everything was coded correctly.
- Once you know all the work has been posted, create customer statements and mail them.
- Make sure the renewals for the upcoming month have been mailed.
- Close the month in the computer so you can start fresh with the next month.
- After the close, produce all reports that tell you exactly where you are and how you've performed.

Checklists can be used for many processes. For example, a valuable checklist would be one to be used at the end of each day for technicians to submit when they come in at night. This determines if everything that was supposed to be covered was covered. This also will point out any follow-ups necessary on the part of a technician, manager or anyone else. Checklists are a great way to alleviate stress. Any structure you can provide is helpful to an employee and organization. You want to make the day boring. Today has to be just like yesterday and the day before so you don't have to reinvent your business every day.

Manage your risk

When it comes to your company's important assets – whether they're computers, trucks or machinery – develop contingency plans and backup resources. When these resources break down, or just take the day off, your business needs to remain running.

Another area that needs to be systematized is your so-called fire drill. What do you do if one of your trucks breaks down? What happens if someone is injured? What are the steps for handling emergencies?

Think about how you're going to approach these daily surprises and how they'll be resolved. Develop protocols to decrease your exposure to risk and bring emergencies to a resolution. This can be a scary business.
Think about it:

- People are up on ladders.
- People crawl through tiny spaces.
- Chemicals are being transported and applied.
- Trucks (and people) are on the road.

Anytime the human element is involved, we're open to risk. To mitigate this, develop a system of protocols and backup plans to get through any unpredictable situation. Put controls on your processes, and make sure they're followed. Then run exercises to ensure your emergency protocols work. Practice, practice, practice! It's just like the common fire drill. It takes practice to make sure everyone understands the procedure and make sure it works in the first place.

Build an employee training process to develop your

homegrown business capability. There are two ways to develop your top-notch workforce. Hire workers with experience and knowledge, which can be expensive, or hire workers without the knowledge and train them to work in your system. The homegrown approach will provide better results because it can be cheaper and you can train your employees to work the way that works best for your organization. It's rare to hire technicians from other service providers and have them adhere to your policies and procedures immediately. There will be the occasional success story, but for the most part, it ends in failure or a tremendous retraining many times.

Delivering service is regimented and process-heavy. Other service professionals have trained their technicians to work a certain way, so it's unlikely those individuals have been trained the way you want them. If you hire technicians who've developed bad habits from previous jobs, it will take a lot of effort and energy to correct the problem, not to mention a lot of time to just find out what the technician did in the first place.

In many instances, a better approach is to take someone who's not from the industry and plug him into your system so you can dictate the kind of attitude you want the technician to have, what he's allowed to do, when he's going to work, how he's going to drive, and so on.

Make sure the people you hire can be trained so you can make them work the system the way you want it worked and you don't end up with a guy who's working against the grain and trying to do things his own way.

Continuity-in-customer-service issues also need to be worked out when an employee leaves or is promoted and another employee is plugged into a route. Customers are used to the way you deliver service, so if a new technician does things differently, the customer might be confused. Perhaps he'll believe the service quality has decreased even if this isn't the case. Make sure your organization is tight in the eyes of your customer and procedures are done uniformly in appearance and fact.

Determine what information and skills your employees need to possess to service your clients well. Prepare guides and materials that will give your workforce the ability to service your clientele well and keep them happy.

Quality is the goal. Your employees are your vehicles. Train your employees to deliver your vision of quality and value.

Promote continued learning

Technicians must be knowledgeable and skilled at providing services. To maintain your greatest asset, your workforce, you must ensure its learning never ends. Technicians must remain informed about new advances in the industry, as well as your company's new processes. It's extremely important to invest in this asset. Send technicians to educational seminars and conferences and have them take advanced service courses. Money spent in this area is a sure bet for a worthwhile return on investment.

If you're going to offer top-notch products and services to your customers, recognize what they are. In a service business, your product is your people, so make sure your employees are the most knowledgeable, best-trained, honest, all-around good people you can find.

In addition to training required by the state in which you operate, consider going above and beyond the minimum requirements with your employees. Other learning opportunities you can provide them include online courses, seminars, conferences, books, CDs and DVDs.

When you train employees, make sure you do it correctly. And make sure they retain the knowledge gained because you're footing the bill.

A good way to do this is make sure technicians know they'll be tested and held accountable after a training seminar or conference. Test them or make them answer questions. Require them to apply their newfound knowledge toward some tangible improvement in the business. You'll find they'll retain much more information this way.

Also, make it clear they'll be held accountable for using the information. This is a reward and an opportunity for employees to move forward in the company. In the end, they'll feel better about themselves when they're trained, and this will help them deliver better quality service to your clients.

Will they leave?

You're educating them, making them better people and more marketable. Other service companies will notice them and make offers to hire the best employees from your company. This is a significant concern for many business owners. Many owners don't want their employees to be marketable, which is the wrong attitude to have.

If employees aren't marketable, why would a customer want them to do the work they need done? You can't keep the job offers away, and you wouldn't want to hold employees back. It's difficult to find good people, and when you do, you want to protect them as much as possible. You also want to do the right thing by treating them well and giving them additional opportunities to develop their careers. But if you're truly good to your employees and pay them well, they won't leave. There might be a few employees who slip away to competitors, but they never get your good people because they realize how good you are to them.

Train your managers

Train your managers to understand the profit and growth objective. Get your management team on board with your company's profit and growth objectives. Make sure your managers understand the vision and have a strong grasp of which metrics are important. Ultimately, you should eliminate the need to manage the business alone; but the only way to do this is develop a management team you can trust to operate and improve the business without you.

Train your technicians about how to perform services in an efficient and profitable manner, and train your office employees to understand how to run a profitable business. They have to consider the financial goal you set out for them every day.

You have to generate a certain amount of revenue each day. You're selling your employees skills, but what you're really selling is their time; and your employees' time is a perishable asset. Once it's gone, you can't get it back. It's like operating a fruit stand. If you don't sell the product, the fruit rots. You don't have a store with a product on the shelf where, if you don't sell that product, it remains on the shelf and you can sell it tomorrow or another time. Time is a perishable item. Once the day ends, unsold time is gone. So, manage your revenue, routes and services hourly and realize every tick of the clock hits your bottom-line profit.

Incentivize your employees

A business owners' motivation is easy to define. Increased business success and profitability equals more cash in owners' pocket; yet, employee motivation is more difficult to create. Develop a clearly defined incentive program that's fair and enticing. Also, build a healthy level of competition among employees.

Offer your salespeople and technicians a commission for sales. Create different incentive plans for everyone from customer service representatives to salespeople to technicians.

Build team spirit and make work fun. Let the company work toward a goal. If employees achieve the goal, they can win a dinner at a fancy restaurant, which can contribute to office morale and camaraderie.

Individual contests are a great way to create healthy competition. There are great ways to run contests and competitions in your office. Develop a point system. When an employee captures a testimonial from a customer, he earns points. When an employee upsells an additional service to a customer, he earns points. When a technician hits all his stops on time, he earns points. When a CSR solves a customer's problem, she earns points. Keeping trucks clean, generating leads for salespeople, wearing uniforms, etc. - you can assign a point value for every desirable behavior you want to encourage. Employees can accumulate points that can be used to order prizes from a catalog you put together.

Here's another twist to the contest idea involving a deck of cards: Instead of points, hand out a playing card for a job well done. At the end of the month, the person with the best poker hand is awarded the prize. It drives people to compete and creates a fun atmosphere in the office.

Recognition is an effective motivator, but there are many ways to recognize achievement in your organization. Post a sales leader board so everyone can see how well others are doing. Distribute a regular newsletter highlighting compliments, big milestones and accomplishments. Give out company awards for the most valuable employee, most improved, best department, etc.

There are many ways to motivate people. It's not only about money, it's about recognizing accomplishments and generating pride.

Effective routing is key to profitability

Optimize your routing to get the most out of your technicians' time. Efficient routing will keep your technicians on site, providing services to your clients for a higher percentage of the time they're available.

Another way to increase the effectiveness of your routes is offering customers a discount for signing up early. This will enable you to schedule more effectively. By booking appointments earlier you'll know in advance how to route the work much more efficiently than if you create the routes on the fly as the work comes in.

Aside from keeping your workforce productive, other

efficient routing benefits include saving gas and decreased wear and tear on your vehicles. Optimized routing benefits are significant and can be quantified as we illustrated in chapter 6.

Collections isn't a four letter word

The goal of a business is to make money. You can bill your clients for your services, but if you never collect the money, it becomes a receivable with no value. Develop a process for collecting money from customers who owe you money, and make it a repeatable process anyone can perform.

This is an area nobody wants to get involved with because the general perception is nothing good can come of it. The best thing that can happen is you get your money that's already owed to you; but more likely, you're going to hear about what a terrible service you provide, or you'll hear a million excuses why they can't pay.

So, that's what you're up against.

Now it's time to collect because you have bills to pay, too; and if they don't pay you, and nobody else did, you'd be out of business and unable to provide the quality services you deliver.

Here's a 10-step approach for collecting:

1. Print each overdue invoice, and put them in a binder that has dividers numbered one through 31.
2. Make a scripted phone call.
3. Call the client for a check.
4. If you don't receive payment, get the client to commit to a follow-up date.
5. Let the client know if you don't receive payment you're going to suspend service or terminate the relationship.
6. Move that invoice to the date you plan to follow-up.
7. On that date, tell him he isn't living up to his end of the agreement.
8. Set up the client for another follow-up call.

9. With each call, get progressively more stern.
10. Turn the client over to collections.

Customer service with a smile

While operating your business, it's important employees maintain a high level of customer service and are empowered to resolve issues with customers. Face it, customers will complain. The objective is to end up with a happy, satisfied client who pays you for your services. The focus must be to continue to provide the best quality you can offer to the client. Think about this quote from Jeff Bezos, the founder and CEO of Amazon.com:

"We see our customers as invited guests to a party, and we are the hosts. It's our job every day to make every important aspect of the customer experience a little bit better."

Improve the customer experience by giving employees a system to follow. If you don't, you're going to put out fires instead of running a business. Develop a process for handling client complaints quickly and fairly. The process should empower lower-level resolution and allow employees to escalate certain issues. Yet, incentivize your workforce to come to a desirable resolution before escalating the issues through the ranks. As the owner, stay out of conflicts, and let your customer service reps handle it. Monitor the situation, or step in later to intervene but let the staff give their best effort first.

Keep your mind on the vision

While managing and maintaining control of daily activities, scan the horizon for future issues or events that might impact your business. Always look down the road to ensure you don't get caught by surprise. Remember your high-level objectives and business vision.

When putting out fires, it's often difficult to be a visionary. You might ask, "Who has time for this stuff?" because there are customers to service and bills to pay. But you have to devote time and attention to this task and be diligent about it.

Stay on top of current trends in the industry by reading trade magazines or business newspapers. Take note of how business is developing, and stay in front of trends, such as technology enhancements. Obtain the education and resources needed to run your business, and keep yourself in the know.

Plan the work and work the plan

Stick to the game plan. It's critical to give your plan time to work and avoid distractions. Remember the saying, "Rome wasn't built in a day." Well, that applies to your business plan. As long as you take your time to plan the work, working the plan shouldn't be difficult.

To execute, make sure you're disciplined enough to follow through and deliver consistent, high-quality services. Without the discipline to keep yourself in line with your processes, there's no point creating protocols in the first place.

Whatever can go wrong, will go wrong. This is Murphy's Law. Things never happen the way you want them to. You'll find you're often chasing a goal. Well, stay with your plan, and don't be so hasty to abort it. Stick to the plan, and monitor your progress and success. It doesn't always feel like it, but in many instances, you're gaining ground whether you realize it or not.

Being in business isn't so much about the destination as the journey. So make sure you have a rewarding trip. It's extremely important to devise your overall plan, then make sure you work and communicate it.

As an aside, it's easy for you to say you're going to work the plan, but employees need incentives to change the business. Communicate with the staff, and make sure they know the company goals and clearly understand your vision. If they don't get it, how can you expect them to carry it out?

Deliver quality. Lather, rinse, repeat.

Deliver your services repeatedly with a consistent level of quality much like the McDonald's approach, which should show you how extremely critical this is. Systematize all aspects of your business. Put all your processes on paper. Set your protocol, and make it so anyone can be trained to deliver the service. Protocol must be specific and detailed so you can reach a level of quality that can be duplicated and delivered throughout the company. Train employees, and adhere to the system's protocol. Follow it repeatedly to work out the kinks. Amateurs work until they get it right, and professionals work until they can't get it wrong.

You might find some customers will be attached to a certain technician, which is common with a small service business. However, you need to change this and create a system in which anybody can service a customer with the same the level of quality. The business can't depend on any one person, whether that person is you or the cleaning guy. The system is the focal point, not the individual.

"I am convinced that nothing we do is more important than hiring and developing people. At the end of the day, you bet on people, not on strategies."

—Larry Bossidy

PEOPLE MANAGEMENT

One thing Peter learned in his business law course was labor issues. He remembered a case study in which an employer was sued by a former employee who made false accusations about the amount of time he worked and the tasks he was hired to perform while employed. The lawsuit resulted in hundreds of thousands of dollars in legal fees and a six-figure settlement with the former employee.

While the employer wasn't wrong, the fact he couldn't produce documentation required to prove the employee was paid properly and he wasn't forced to perform job functions inconsistent with his job was to difficult to prove. It was agreed the six-figure settlement was the cheapest way out.

What a shame. If he had the proper documentation, he could have saved himself a lot of time, aggravation and money.

Peter asked Michael how the company hired and retained good employees and what records they kept. Michael was embarrassed as he explained they usually hire friends or friends of friends, and most of the agreements are done with handshakes.

Dan's observations and recommendations

I've observed many successful and unsuccessful companies. The key characteristic common to all successful operations can be summed up in one word – management. In the service business, it's all about managing people. If you start out as a one-man operation, managing people is easy because you only need to manage yourself. As your organization grows, you have to manage technicians, salespeople and office staff. Good employees are your greatest assets in the service business because companies don't offer a product. They offer people and their expertise. A company that offers a good product can sometimes be successful with marginal people based on the merits of the product alone. Service professionals can't do that. The product is the people.

Attracting good people

So how do you attract and retain good people? Well, as much as I hate to admit it, pest control and lawn care industries aren't glamorous businesses. However, if you can demonstrate this type of work provides a good living, a pleasant work environment, and the ability to grow professionally and financially, you should be able to attract good people. But this is much easier said than done.

People want to earn a decent wage, and to attract good people, you need to offer benefits such as 401k and family health insurance. People are motivated by factors that promote self-esteem, and these factors include technical training for job function and financial incentives such as performance-based commissions and bonuses. People feel worthy when they earn extra money for a job well done. Extra money in an employee's pocket is satisfying because it helps pay the bills, but performance-based compensation is a form of recognition of a job well done and just as important.

In a service business, systems must be in place to manage workflow along with accurate accounting of employee incentive-based compensation. Nothing is more demoralizing to employees than not meeting the promise of the aforementioned work environment and incentives only to find a dysfunctional workforce with no systems in place to calculate incentive-based pay programs. There's no faster way to lose a good employee than to cheat him out of pay intentionally or unintentionally because of a lack of systems to calculate and pay those commissions and bonuses promised to him.

Job descriptions

Job descriptions, which are essential in any organization, are required for recruitment so you and the applicants can understand their role. A job description defines a person's role and accountability. Without a job description, it's not possible for a person to properly commit to, or be held accountable for a role. Job descriptions improve an organization's ability to manage people and roles in the following ways:

- Clarifies employer expectations for the employee.
- Provides a basis of measuring job performance.
- Provides a clear description of the role for job candidates.

- Provides a structure and discipline for a company to understand and structure all jobs, as well as ensure necessary activities, duties and responsibilities are covered by one job or another.
- Enables pay and grading systems to be structured fairly and logically.
- Essential reference tool when employee/employer disputes arise.
- Essential reference tool for discipline.
- Provides important reference points for training and development areas.
- Enables an organization to structure and manage roles in a uniform way, thus increasing efficiency of recruitment, training and workflow.

In a pest control or lawn care company, the following jobs are essential. However, with a small company, there might be multiple job descriptions performed by one person, who might be part or full time. With a large company, there might be additional jobs required. The essential jobs required are:

- Service technician
- Salesperson
- Customer service representative (CSR)
- Bookkeeper
- Manager

Be clear on what you're hiring for. A clearly defined job description is a good start toward ensuring your recruiting efforts stay on track and the end result is a desirable one. The following is a sample outline for a thorough, well-written job posting.

    I.   Title of the position
    II.   Department the position is under

III. Direct line of report (who's the boss?)
IV. General and specific areas of responsibility
V. Who the person will interact with regularly
VI. Term of employment if applicable
VII. Overall qualifications (required skills
and experience)

Once an applicant joins the team, a job description can become an informal agreement about what the expectations of the employee are. This provides accountability and can describe what you want a candidate to accomplish in terms of achieving your definition of success.

Help-wanted ads

Take your time writing your help-wanted ad. Put some thought into writing a help wanted ad. So many people publish generic classified ads that say nothing special – and they wonder why the people who respond aren't special. Take your time, and write a help-wanted ad as if you were advertising to your customers. Be specific, indicate the benefits of the job, and be clear about what you're looking for.

The people you hire will be the face of your organization, and you're only as good as your help, so take hiring seriously. Have a system in place where you advertise the position, select candidates to interview, and interview them thoroughly. Writing an effective help wanted ad, which will drive people into your recruiting funnel, is the first step to give your company a shot at finding the right people.

Think about the following when you advertise a job opportunity:

• **Sell, sell, sell.** Many people don't think of recruiting as a sales activity, but it is. There are many positions, so why should a candidate choose your position over the others?

Make sure your ad portrays the benefits of the job, not just what you need from a candidate.

- **Grab the attention of the market.** Using creative headlines, make sure the title and description jump off the page. You want your ad to pop so you get the most mileage out of your recruiting dollars.
- **Your job is unique.** Consider what's special about the job. If it weren't special, why would an outstanding candidate apply? If your ad describes a job that's a one-of-a-kind, wonderful opportunity, readers will be even more attracted.
- **Help foster vision.** Spend the majority of your ad here, explaining what a day in the life would look like should this candidate get the job. Advertise your vision of the job, and hopefully your soon-to-be employees will share that vision.
- **Be specific.** Keep your list of needs short, and be specific when explaining the qualifications of the position. Make sure you get what you're looking for and expectations are aligned.
- **Get the ad out now.** Don't wait until you need a new employee to publish your ad. If you wait until an emergency happens, you're bound to whatever comes in.

The right people

Make sure you're familiar with the job description for which you're hiring. Review applications or resumes with a fine-toothed comb, weeding out any blatantly unqualified candidates. Keep the job description in mind, and be aware of what you're hiring for. Skills and experience are key, but a candidate's personality also can tell you a lot. Make sure the applicant will fit in with the rest of your team and help the organization achieve its goals.

In addition, think about your business objectives. What kind of role will this individual play in your daily routine?

Think of what the position is, but more importantly, the type of person you want to fill the position. If you want your technicians to be able to sell, look for a balance of skills. A candidate might make the best technician, but if you're also looking for someone who can upsell your programs, then you might not be looking for the typical technician. You might be looking for someone who has other abilities than the typical technician skill requirements.

Furthermore, when seeking the perfect employees, you'll come across many not-so-perfect candidates. There are many caution signs you might find in a candidate's resume. Here's a list of resume items that should indicate warning flags:

1. **Gaps in employment** might hint at a number of things, the most concerning of which is perhaps nobody else wanted to hire this person. Is there something you're missing? Any gaps have to be explained.
2. **Job jumping** is a big warning sign. Individuals who jump from job to job can be a big headache. Turnover is expensive, so why take on an employee who has made a living contributing to turnover?
3. **Typos and grammatical errors** show the applicant didn't put forth his best effort and might not be that interested in the job.
4. **Was that his first job?** Sometimes a candidate's first job listed on the resume is a high-level position, which means he probably didn't list all his work experience. Have him fill in the blanks for you.
5. **The general look and feel** of the resume can tell you a lot. Does the person seem well organized? Is the resume awkward? Perhaps it's boring.
6. **If the education credentials don't list a degree**, can you be sure the candidate graduated?
7. **The applicant is overqualified (and he knows it).** Why would a candidate want to take a job beneath his skill

and experience level? There's a feeling of desperation here, which is concerning.

If possible, ask for and check an applicant's references before granting an interview. This will save you time weeding out any candidates whose information doesn't match their references. Furthermore, you might gain valuable information from previous employers that will aid you in making your decision. Take all information with a grain of salt because there might be history between the applicant and his references of which you're unaware.

Many employers don't check references, which is foolish. Why would you pass on an opportunity to find out about a person you're about to welcome into your business.

This should be a mandatory requirement. Develop a system through which you check references. Many people will give you only a former employee's start date, end date and the name of the position held. Others will open the floodgates of information and provide you with more information than you could gather in an interview.

But you never know until you ask, so check references methodically. The following are sample questions that can be asked of references to help you to gather vital information:

- Are you agreeable to sharing information about this candidate and his work history?
- Which roles or job titles did the candidate maintain in your organization?
- In your opinion, were the candidate's duties performed well?
- Does the candidate work better on teams or alone?
- Does the candidate deal well with stress?
- Can you provide specific examples of the candidate's accomplishments?
- Can you describe specific instances in which the

candidate performed below expectations?
- Would you hire this person again? If so, why? If not, why?
- Would you feel comfortable recommending this candidate for this position?

Make sure you gather all the facts and read between the lines.

The interview is your last chance to gather information about an applicant before making a hiring decision. Once you decide to hire someone, it's difficult to fire them.

When you go into an interview, know your objectives and have a plan. This isn't a casual conversation. During an interview, you must gather all the facts so you can make a well-informed decision. Before the interview, make sure you're familiar with the applicant's background and prepare questions that will get you to the information you're looking for. Here are examples:

- **Trait:** honesty and integrity
- **Question:** Give me an example of a time when you displayed honesty or integrity at work.
- **Trait:** excellent attendance and dependability
- **Question:** When we call your previous employer or references, what are they likely to tell us about your dependability and attendance?
- **Trait:** Team oriented
- **Question:** Do you work best with others or alone? Provide an example of a time when you have shown this.
- **Trait:** Detail orientated
- **Question:** Specifically explain how you improved a task or job on which you were working.
- **Trait:** Strong work ethic
- **Question:** Describe an instance when you went above and beyond your responsibility to complete a task.

Also, if you plan to have more than one person interview a candidate during the course of the day, plan a structured schedule. You don't want candidates lingering around your office feeling lost. Additionally, don't lose control of the agenda. Control the process from start to finish, within each interview and during every gap in between.

Also, if you're planning to have more than one person interview an applicant, split up the work. Determine beforehand who will ask which questions to gain what information. This will make your interview process efficient and effective.

Lead the interview

Going into an interview, your only objective is to gain as much pertinent information as possible. You have specific questions and need detailed information. The only way to make sure candidates talk about what you need them to talk about is by leading the conversation down the path you want it to go. If you left it up to the interviewee to lead the discussion, then you'll never learn about all the reasons why you don't want to hire the person. You have to ask specific questions.

The objective is to learn as much as you can about this person in a fairly brief period of time. It's like a game of Twenty Questions. Your questions have to be efficient and effective. Develop your set of precise questions.

Offer the applicant a few minutes at the end of the interview to ask questions. But, until that moment, every second leading up to the final Q&A is your time, not theirs. Fire off all the questions you wanted to ask, and collect as many answers as you can.

A strong set of interviewing skills might improve your chances of uncovering hidden talent and skill. Yet, no amount of interviewing skill can make poor candidates into good ones. A handful of these solid candidates make all the difference for your company.

Do background checks on your job applicants. Look at criminal and driving records (there are services online) and employment history. Look for obvious blemishes on criminal records, as well as people who make a living jumping from job to job-faking injuries. Contact your insurance companies, including your auto and liability carriers. You might find they'll do such investigations, or they might provide you with sources that can perform the inquiry for less money because it's in their best interest. Employing good drivers means fewer accidents. Also, it seems simple, but you want people who aren't criminals in your customers' homes. Your insurance company feels the same way, so your interests are aligned with the insurance companies'. Use that to your advantage, and let them help you with an applicant's background check.

Unfortunately, passing on an opportunity to do a background check can leave you open to liabilities. It's important you take a look at the backgrounds of your technicians, especially because they'll be entering the homes of your clients. If you skip the background check and the employee is involved in harmful misconduct or illegal activity, you might be liable for negligent hiring or retention.

Compensation-level consistency

Put your employees on a consistent compensation track, which will ensure there's equality and fairness when cutting paychecks. This also will help you maintain morale among the ranks.

The evaluation process must be standardized and consistently administered. If done correctly, this procedure fosters fairness and motivation in the workplace. You can't have special deals on the side for certain people. Put people in a system, and through periodic performance evaluations, gauge each employee's success accomplishing their objectives. Changes in compensation levels will often arise out of the performance review process. Keep the reviews performance based, and ensure your personal opinions and emotional input are checked at the door. Refrain from the personal and behavioral aspects of their job.

When completing evaluations, make certain everything is black and white. Also collect all the facts needed to do the performance review thoroughly. A review should be consistent. Based on the evaluations, reward employees based on their production and performance. You might not like everybody you work with, but you have to put those emotions aside. If employees perform their job according to your standards, and they do it consistently well, you have to reward them. Make sure rewards are justifiable, and compensation is kept within a reasonable standard.

Some employees will come into your office during peak season and request more money. An effective way to defend this tactic is to keep a bench of part-time technicians ready who are willing to do an occasional job and help you out in a jam. The message you want to deliver is no one is above the company, which won't be crippled if someone leaves. Everyone is replaceable, and that's the beauty of this concept.

Create accountability and apply progressive discipline when needed. Guide your employees' behavior by establishing metrics and goals that are reviewed and graded during periodic performance reviews. This is a great exercise for creating accountability. Additionally, if it comes to the point where you have to fire someone, it's wise to implement progressive discipline so you can build a case against that employee.

When things head south, be sure the situation is reflected in performance reviews and other forms of feedback. Discuss the specifics, and document them. Building a case against an employee can be a long and tedious process, but if you're going to let someone go, things will be much smoother if you go through this exercise and take your time to collect a file of poor performance reviews and customer complaints. You're doing yourself and your employees a huge disservice by not addressing issues immediately.

Aside from being a tool used to serve an underperforming employee, progressive discipline can be used as an employee development tactic. If you progressively alert people and give them feedback, you can work toward developing your employees more. You'll see they're happier and feel more connected to your expectations. Sometimes, it's also a good way for employees to remain grounded and tuned in to the company. With more feedback, retention will increase and turnover will decrease.

Many times, your best employees will receive positive reviews. Make sure you give them a pat on the back so they feel good about themselves.

Every once in a while, there will be an employee who steps out of line, but this doesn't always indicate a need to fire that person immediately. Develop a consistent and reliable yardstick by which your employees' actions will be measured. Repercussions also must be consistent and administered swiftly.

Discipline in the workforce is important. Having a formal and consistent policy for discipline will make your actions effective and fair. When you sit down with an underperforming employee, the tone needs to be serious and the conversation needs to focus on factual specifics. There's no place for emotion. Explain the bad behavior that doesn't sit well with you and how the situation needs to be remedied. Align expected improvements and necessary actions with behavioral problems. Detail the results you anticipate from the employee and the time through which improvement is required. Stay focused, and don't stray from the facts. Sit the employee down and explain you're dissatisfied with his performance. Explain that if the situation doesn't improve over a short period of time (e.g. 30 days), you'll be forced to let him go. Document the discussion in a memo, provide him a copy, and add it to his file. Sometimes this action alone will be enough to ignite extra effort in your lackluster employees.

Time to go

Nobody likes firing people. OK, maybe some people like firing people. But let's face it, most don't. Every now and then, it just comes to a point where an employee is hurting the organization, and you're not left with any option but to let the employee go before he causes too much damage to the asset that's your livelihood. Knowing where to draw the line can be difficult, but knowing when an employee has crossed that line is the tricky part. Consider:

- **Keeping it short and sweet.** OK, at least make it short. Avoid getting caught up in emotions or long-winded explanations. Tell the employee he's being terminated, the reason why, and the terms that go along with it.
- **Making a clean break.** There's no reason for the employee to stick around. Tell him to pack and leave the premises immediately. Be sure he turns in any company property, including credit cards, keys, etc.
- **Reassigning responsibilities quickly.** Now that someone has left the office, there likely will be a gap to fill. Reassign his duties to other employees so your business doesn't miss a beat.
- **Swinging the ax.** Get it done. The most harmful thing to your organization is if you don't fire a poorly performing or disgruntled employee and let him hang around. This is like poisoning your staff with unneeded negativity and will damage team morale.

It's critical to organize and continue collecting detailed employee records. It's been said if you hang around long enough, you're going to be successful. Unfortunately, if you hang around long enough, you're going to be sued. So, it's important to keep detailed records of any interaction between you and the terminated employee, which can be effective if you stay on top of it. There are software packages that can do this for you as well. Items you want to keep in each employee's file are:

- Form W-4 (employment withholding information)
- Form W-2 (wage and tax statement – save all years)
- Form I-9 (employment eligibility form)
- Pesticide applicator license
- Driver's license
- Social Security card
- Original job application
- Resume submitted when applying for the position
- Reference checks (from previous employers)
- Background checks (including criminal and driving records)
- Drug testing results
- Any written communication with employee during employment (such as performance reviews and/or complaints)
- Compensation history (how much you paid the employee and dates when you gave raises and/or bonuses)
- Customer comments (praise and complaints)

All other items relevant to your employees and their work history with your company should be added to their file. Make sure all your information and systems are well organized and ready. The value of thorough preparation for future events can't be stressed enough.

"Success is going from failure to failure without a loss of enthusiasm."
—*Winston Churchill*

YOUR NEXT STEPS

Passing a business to the next generation is always a difficult decision for a first-generation entrepreneur, but Michael has seen his son grow and grasp many of the concepts needed to take a business from an owner operation to a professionally managed business, which is separate from the owner, that can sustain itself, grow and provide a well-earned retirement for its founder. Peter has validated the recurring revenue business model for his future. He needs to devise a plan to create policies and procedures that will document how the business is to be run and create a road map for growth and success.

Dan's observations and recommendations

The service industry is full of opportunity and profitability. It's easy to make money in this business. If you've read this book, you've clearly chosen a new path for your service business. You've chosen to follow a path of more profitability, increased productivity and maximum personal reward.

Keep this book handy whenever you find yourself in a jam. If you slide off track, refer to this book to put you back on track. Maybe some of the material hits home for you; maybe some of the material will hit home for you in the future. Wherever you are, know you're not alone. There are thousands of service professionals just like you learning to manage and grow their business. Remember, it's all about the journey, so make sure you have fun and enjoy your experience. Life is too short not to.